He cupped the si[de of her face in his] hand and lowered his head. His lips brushed hers, light at first but then his mouth parted, an indication he wanted to deepen the kiss. She slipped her arms around his neck and pulled him closer to her. She'd never kissed a man in a wooded area. The smells from the trees, the hint of fall in the air, the cool air around them. She'd experienced none of this before while with a man. This was all new to her. And since it was new, it was something she wanted to explore. There was no better place to make love.

Before she had time to think through her next move, she unbuttoned his pants. If he didn't think about it, maybe he'd finally consummate their marriage. She wanted to do this. She wanted to do this in the secluded area, surrounded by nothing but trees and the blue sky above them.

"Make love to me, Al," she whispered. "Make me your wife. Please?"

"Are you sure?" he asked, even as she knew his erection had to be pressing him to do as she requested.

Her gaze went to his and she noted the glimmer of hope in his eyes. He wanted to be intimate with her, had wanted it from the time they got married. But even while he'd wanted it, he held back for her sake. He loved her. She mattered to him. It wouldn't be a quick and meaningless act. It would draw him closer to her, and she wanted that more than she wanted anything.

"I'm sure, Al," she whispered. "I've never been more sure of anything in my life."

***

The Mail Order Bride's Deception

The Mail Order Bride's Deception

Ruth Ann Nordin

Wedded Bliss Romances, LLC

This is a work of fiction. The events and characters described herein are imaginary and are not intended to refer to specific places or living persons. The opinions expressed in this manuscript are solely the opinions of the author and also represent the opinions or thoughts of the publisher.

The Mail Order Bride's Deception
All Rights Reserved.
Copyright 2014 Ruth Ann Nordin
V1.0

Cover Photo Image Dreamstime. www.dreamstime.com Al rights reserved – used with permission.

Interior Photo image Dreamstime. www.dreamstime.com All right reserved – used with permission.

This book may not be reproduced, transmitted, or stored in whole or in part by any means including graphic, electronic, or mechanical without expressed written consent of the publisher/author except in the case of brief quotations embodied in critical articles and reviews.

Dedication: To Debra MacArthur who is a lot of fun. You are a very sweet lady!

List of Romances by Ruth Ann Nordin

Regencies

<u>Marriage by Scandal</u>
The Earl's Inconvenient Wife
A Most Unsuitable Earl
His Reluctant Lady
The Earl's Scandalous Wife

<u>Standalone Regency</u>
Her Counterfeit Husband

Historical Westerns

<u>Nebraska Romance Collection</u>
Her Heart's Desire
A Bride for Tom
A Husband for Margaret
Eye of the Beholder
The Wrong Husband
Shotgun Groom
To Have and To Hold
His Redeeming Bride
Isaac's Decision

<u>South Dakota Romance Collection</u>
Loving Eliza
Bid for a Bride
Bride of Second Chances

<u>Montana Romance Collection</u>
Mitch's Win
Boaz's Wager

<u>Wild Hearts Series</u> (Co-Written with Stephannie Beman)
The Stagecoach Bride

<u>Historical Romantic Anthology</u> (Co-Written with Janet Syas Nitsick)
Bride by Arrangement

Native American Romance Series
Restoring Hope
A Chance In Time (novella)
Brave Beginnings
Bound by Honor, Bound by Love

Virginia Romance Collection
An Unlikely Place for Love
The Cold Wife
An Inconvenient Marriage
Romancing Adrienne

Standalone Historical Westerns
Falling In Love With Her Husband
Kent Ashton's Backstory
Catching Kent
Meant To Be

Contemporaries

Omaha Contemporary Romances
With This Ring, I Thee Dread
What Nathan Wants

Florida Contemporary Romances
Substitute Bride

Across the Stars Series
Suddenly a Bride
Runaway Bride
His Abducted Bride

Chapter One

Rapid City, Dakota Territory
September 1878

Sadie Miller's heart raced with trepidation as she looked at the letter in her hands from the man who waited for his mail-order bride. She couldn't read it. The ticket master had read it to her when she ordered her train ticket. It was from a man named Allen Grover who lived in Rapid City, and he had a six-month-old son named Gilbert. From what she gathered, he lived off the land. Occasionally he sold meat to the town butcher, but he mostly bartered for things he needed and either grew or killed his own food.

Allen sounded like a nice man, the kind of man she could enjoy spending the rest of her life with. Hazel had said he was the kind of man who'd be good to her. Then she gave Sadie her drawstring purse with the money, letter, and ticket. Even now, as Sadie held the woman's things, she couldn't help the mixture of feelings that the items provoked. What happened to Hazel had been horrible, but it had been the very thing that freed her. This was her chance. A new start. A new life. A chance to put the past behind her.

She peered through the small window of the stagecoach as it came to a stop. Her gaze passed over a couple of men before she found one who was holding a baby in one arm. He was in front of the mercantile and he was a handsome man. Tan from hours spent outdoors, about six feet tall, light brown hair peeking out from under his hat, and a muscular build from hard work. He wore a pair of denims and a faded blue and white plaid shirt that had seen better days. Yes, that had to be him. No other man had a child with him.

She took a deep breath. When she stepped out of this stagecoach, she would be Hazel McPherson. Not Sadie Miller. She closed her eyes for a moment and reminded herself that she could do this. She had to do this. Because if she didn't…

Well, it was better if she didn't think about it.

She adjusted her hat and patted her auburn hair which she had pulled back into a bun. Except for an errant curl that fell from the pins, everything was in place. Keeping the letter out, she closed the drawstring purse and prepared to get out. The moment she set foot on the dirt road, she would be Hazel.

The driver opened the door and held his hand out to help her down. She accepted it. Her legs shook as she took her first tentative step forward. This was it. There was no going back. Daring a glance at the young man, her steps slowed when she realized he was already heading in her direction.

Her heartbeat picked up. Would he believe she was Hazel? Did Hazel tell him what she looked like in one of her letters? Did she look enough like Hazel for him to think it was her? Hazel had brown hair with golden highlights, not the reddish tint she did. And she'd been thinner and taller than Sadie. But why would Hazel mention something like that? She might mention her hair color, maybe even her eye color, but she probably wouldn't go further than that.

"Are you Miss Hazel McPherson?" the young man asked.

Her gaze went to the sleeping child in his arms before going back to him. Nodding, she offered a hopeful smile. "Yes." She held out the letter to him. "Are you Allen Grover?"

"I am, but you can call me Al." With a glance at the letter, he chuckled. "And I wrote that letter. I'd recognize my sloppy handwriting anywhere."

She laughed at his joke. "I had no trouble figuring out what the letter said."

"You're one of the few." He motioned to the stagecoach where the driver and gunman were tying the horses to a post. "Don't you have any luggage?"

"Oh." Luggage? "Um, well..." She turned back to him. "I wanted a fresh start. I thought I'd make my own clothes, especially since the weather is supposed to be colder here."

Thank goodness she'd taken the time to listen to the couple who spent their whole time chatting about the Black Hills before they got off three hours ago. But that was neither here nor there. At the moment, she had more pressing things to deal with.

"I brought some money for the clothes," she assured Al. Judging by what he was wearing, he didn't have much to his name, and the last thing she wanted him to do was change his mind and not marry her—or rather Hazel.

"I was afraid I scared you when I warned you about how cold it can get out here in the winter," he said as he took her by the arm and led her up the platform in front of the mercantile. "I know it's nothing like Atlanta."

She had no idea what Atlanta was like, so she'd just have to take his word for it. "I appreciated the warning," she ventured, hoping it was the right thing to say. "I like to be prepared." Especially after everything she'd been through. "I don't like surprises."

"You won't get any from here. There's not much to do. I hope you don't get bored."

"Boredom is the least of my concerns." In fact, she welcomed it. The quiet blessedness of boredom would be wonderful! Peaceful even.

"You might be saying otherwise after being here a month."

He shot her a smile that threatened to melt her right on the spot. She had a weakness for dimples and he had such cute ones. And his green eyes with brown flecks around the pupils twinkled, hinting at the joy in his life. Such joy had eluded her for quite some time. It would certainly be nice to be surrounded by it again.

It was on the tip of her tongue to ask about his first wife but she decided against it. Hazel probably knew the details, and if she asked the wrong questions, he'd know she wasn't the woman he expected her to be.

Choosing a safer question, she asked, "May I hold Gilbert?"

"Of course."

They stopped and he placed Gilbert in her arms. Afraid she might hurt him, she was careful as she brought him closer to her. He opened his eyes and glanced back at his father before turning his large brown eyes to her. She offered the boy a tentative smile, wondering if babies picked up on an adult's uncertainty. All he did was stare up at her as if he'd never seen a woman before.

She knew nothing about caring for babies or children and had no idea if Hazel did or not. But even so, she guessed that each child was different, just as every person was different. She was going to be his mother now. The sooner she got used to him, the better.

She brushed back one of his blond curls. "He's got lovely hair."

"Yes, he does."

Did Gilbert take after his first mother? Unfortunately, Al decided not to divulge anything. He resumed his walk and started telling her where stores were in the town. Despite her curiosity, she didn't press him for more information. For all she knew, he'd told Hazel everything already so why would he repeat himself? Besides, he was taking her as his second wife, and that being the case, he'd want to focus on her.

Pushing aside the stab of guilt in her gut, she forced her attention to what he was saying. Hazel was dead. There was no bringing her back. And that being the case, all she was doing was filling in for her. Yes, it was a lie. Yes, she was deceiving him. But what harm could possibly come from it? It wasn't like anyone from Nebraska was going to come up here to visit Hazel.

"I spent the better part of the day getting the cabin ready for you," Al said.

"A cabin?"

"I told you it's only got two bedrooms. I know you're used to a large home with servants at your beck and call. This won't be anything like that." His steps slowed. "Are you sure you want to go through with this? Once we marry, it's forever."

Hazel came from a large home with servants? Sadie had no idea this was the case based on the simple clothing Hazel wore. But Hazel did have a lot of money in her drawstring purse. Just what had Hazel's life been like, and why would she leave such luxury to come out here?

"Hazel?" Al asked, drawing her attention back to him.

"I'm sorry. I got distracted." No sense in telling him why. "What is it?"

"I was asking you if you're sure you want to marry me. Life out here isn't an easy one. There are bitter winters. You'll have to cook, clean, and sew. Now, I meant what I said. I want you here, and Aunt Betty is more than happy to teach you what you need to know. But it's hard work, especially when you have a child to tend to. You've led such a sheltered life. I'm just not sure you're up to it."

She thought over his words with interest. "You accepted my reply to your mail-order bride advertisement." Or rather,

Hazel's reply. "Forgive me if you mentioned it and I forgot, but did you not get any other replies?"

"I didn't mention it," he quietly replied. "Because no other replies came. I had sent out the ad when Gilbert was born."

So that's why he jumped at the chance at marrying Hazel. She was the only one who answered and he had a child who needed a mother. Well, she was nothing like Hazel. Her life hadn't been one of luxury. She'd had to learn to fight and struggle to survive. She'd known hunger, pain, and loneliness. These were things Hazel had rescued her from.

"Hazel?"

Tears she'd learned to suppress threatened to expose her weakness. She quickly blinked them away. She focused on the man standing in front of her and the child in her arms. This was a new beginning. A new start. She could do this.

"Hard work and cold winters don't scare me," she told him.

There were worse things out there. Monsters that took the form of men. She rubbed Gilbert's back and looked at Al. He wasn't a monster. He was a good man—an honest man. And he was desperate for a wife who'd be a mother to his son.

"I want to marry you, Al. I wouldn't have come all this way if I didn't. It might take me some time to get used to being here, but I will. I promise you that."

He relaxed and smiled. "I wouldn't have blamed you if you wanted to leave after you saw this place, but I'm glad you're staying."

She returned his smile, assured that he really would have let her leave if that was what she wanted. No man had given her a choice before. It was nice to control her destiny for a change. "I am, too."

"I told the preacher we'd stop by his house to get married if you wanted to stay. He lives right down that way."

She followed his gaze to the dusty road lined with small houses that weren't far from the few businesses in the town.

"We can gather the items you need from the mercantile first or wait until after the wedding."

Surprised he was giving her another choice, she said, "We're closer to the mercantile so we might as well go there now."

With a nod, he directed her to the mercantile and they bought the supplies they needed. He asked her what she wanted, but she couldn't recall much about cooking so she left it up to him and requested the recipe book on the counter.

She was close to telling him how inadequate she was in the kitchen, but when he told her, "I suppose since you had servants, you didn't cook," she relaxed. Good. He didn't expect Hazel to be good at making food. That gave her some leeway as she adjusted to her new life. When it came time for her to select cloth to make dresses, she picked the blue fabric with small white polka dots on it.

"Do you want to pick another one?" he asked, gesturing to the green, gray, and yellow colors.

"Well," she slowly began as she tried to determine which colors didn't somehow remind her of her past. The blue was a given. It was for proper ladies. Red and purple wouldn't do because she'd worn those colors often. Green, gray, and yellow were colors she could associate with other things. The rug on the floor, the drapes covering the windows, or the suit *he'd* wear. Finally, she said, "I'll pick the yellow one." At least she hadn't stared at the rug for hours on end.

After he paid for the fabrics and the supplies she needed, the owner helped Al carry the crates out to his wagon. Sadie looked down at the baby in her arms. He rested his head on her shoulder and fell back to sleep. Still not used to holding a child, she gingerly patted his back. He was going to be her son. She wondered if Hazel was used to children, small or big. So far, she'd lucked out. Hazel hadn't cooked, and given her wealth, she hadn't sewed a lot either. But was she familiar with children? Well, she'd find out soon enough.

Al returned to her and took Gilbert into his arms. "He likes you."

"How can you tell that?" she asked as they headed for the preacher's house.

"He fell asleep while you were holding him. He doesn't do that unless he likes someone." With a grin, he glanced her way. "I don't want to be too forward, but I think that's a sign we're going to have a good marriage."

"Oh." Unsure of how else to respond, she chuckled. He was teasing her, she knew, but he was also hinting at something he believed about Hazel. If she could imitate her well enough, then he was probably right. For sure, he wouldn't have said the same thing about her as Sadie if he knew about her past.

They spent the rest of the walk to the preacher's in silence. At one point, she considered apologizing to him and leaving. But he needed a mother for the little boy and she needed a new start. Hazel wasn't alive and no other woman was willing to come here. She wasn't one who'd usually say fate was at play in her life, but in this situation, there was nothing else to explain it.

She would marry him and spend the rest of her life being a good and faithful wife. She had a feeling he'd be an easy man to live with. Already he was kinder than any others she'd known. Far out in the Black Hills, no one would ever find out the truth. She could slip into the role of wife and mother, and the rest of her life would finally be one of peace.

Chapter Two

During the vows, Al couldn't stop staring at the woman who'd come all the way out to this wilderness to be his wife. She was beautiful. Almost like a fine porcelain doll he'd only seen once in his life when he was a child. Her skin was smooth and white from lack of sunlight. Given her station in life up to now, she didn't have a need to go outside and work where she'd risk a sunburn. It was a shame that being out here would ruin her flawless skin. The summer days would get too hot for her to keep a hat on while she washed laundry outdoors in the stream behind the cabin. Or when she'd have to tend to the gardens or animals. Sooner or later, the sun would have its way with her.

But she'd still have the rosiest lips he'd ever seen on a lady. Her mouth was slightly turned into a frown, but it was really adorable. When she smiled, the whole world seemed to light up around her. Her light blue eyes held a world of mystery in them. There was only so much she could reveal in letters, and since they'd only exchanged two, they had much more to learn about each other. He looked forward to discovering who she was and sharing with her who he was. From the moment he saw her step off the stagecoach, he knew she was meant for him, that they would carve out a life and a home to raise Gilbert and more children in.

It was with great joy that he kissed her after the preacher pronounced them husband and wife. The simple ceremony wasn't anything that she would have gotten back in Atlanta. Back there, she'd undoubtedly have a luxurious bridal gown, fine music and wine, an assortment of foods, and many guests to wish her a happy and long life.

In fact, from this moment on, her life would be much different. She'd have to work hard and learn to cook and sew. It'd be a hard and difficult life for her. He could only guess what the transition would be like. She didn't seem like the weak type of woman who couldn't handle a challenge. If anything, she had the look of a survivor in her, one who could face any obstacle and find a way to overcome it. She'd need that ability out here if she was going to survive. But he'd do his part to make her as comfortable as possible.

After they left the preacher's house, she asked to hold Gilbert again so he obliged her.

He pointed to the tall trees to the north of town. "My cabin is out that way. We're about a half hour out, so you can walk to town if you need to." Before she thought he wasn't going to let her take the horse, he added, "But you're welcome to ride in on a horse if you like. I don't know if you're familiar with riding horses. I mean, I know you mentioned that your father had them, but you never mentioned if you rode them or not. But then, we don't have good riding areas in the forests around here. I don't know if you'll want to go to town by yourself or if you want me to come along." Realizing he was rambling, he added, "Well, you'll figure it all out now that you're here. But if you have any questions, don't hesitate to ask. I want you to feel at home here."

She rubbed the sleeping boy's back and smiled. "It's a nice place. Ideal, even."

He wondered what she meant by that, but then they reached the wagon and he helped her up, placing one hand on her waist as he held her hand. A slight heat crept up his cheeks at the physical contact. Granted, she was now his wife, but they didn't really know each other.

Once she was settled on the wooden seat, he went to the other side and hopped up beside her. He glanced at Gilbert. The poor boy needed a mother in the worst way. Aunt Betty was a wonderful woman, very nurturing and always willing to help out at a moment's notice. But she wasn't his mother.

"I didn't realize you were so good with babies," he told her as he released the wagon's brake.

"You didn't?" she asked.

"You didn't mention anything about taking care of children in your letters."

"Oh." She rubbed the boy's back then she chuckled. "You'll think it's silly, but I don't remember much of what I wrote. What with all the things I had to do to get ready for the trip…" She cleared her throat. "It's been overwhelming but good."

"I understand." He urged the horses forward and proceeded down the dusty road. "I had the easy part. All I had to do was wait for you."

She nodded and turned her attention to the hills around them.

They spent the next couple of minutes in silence. Now that they'd taken care of getting her the things she needed and going to the preacher, she was probably as uncertain of what to say as he was.

They traveled along the bend that took them out of town, and he ventured to joke, "You'll get sick of trees before the year ends."

As he hoped, she laughed. "I love them."

"Yes, but they're all over the place. If you want to see the sun, you have to look up."

"There's nothing wrong with that. I think it's a cozy kind of feeling out here."

"What was Atlanta like? Did you have trees like this?"

Her smile faltered a bit and he wondered about it, but then Gilbert squirmed in her arms and she turned her gaze to him. "I think he's waking up."

"He usually takes a nap earlier in the day, but I think with all the excitement he made himself stay up longer. He probably wanted to see his new ma."

"I can't blame him for being curious." She bit her lower lip in the most adorable way then asked, "Will he be hungry?"

Nodding, he slowed the horses to a stop and turned to the bag he placed under the wooden seat. "I keep a bottle under here." He pulled it out and handed it to her. "Before we came into town, I had him in the bassinet, but I put it back there," he gestured to the back of the wagon, "so that you had a place to put your feet."

She looked over her shoulder. "I didn't notice it before. You certainly are prepared."

"I learned pretty quick that I had to be. Thankfully, Aunt Betty raised some children so she had everything I needed."

Her eyebrows furrowed and he thought she was going to ask him a question but then she smiled. "That's good." She held the bottle up. "Um, as you guessed, I don't have experience with babies. Do I just put it up to his mouth?"

"He knows what to do. This is the easy part. Just wait until I teach you how to change his diaper."

She placed the nipple to the boy's mouth, and he started to drink the goat's milk. "A diaper?"

"The bad news is, sometimes it smells worse than a skunk that got scared and sprayed all over the place, but he no longer pees on people when they change his diaper so that's good."

Her jaw dropped. "You're jesting?"

"No. When he was younger, he'd pee every time I had to change his diaper. Aunt Betty suggested I open the diaper then quickly put it back in place and wait for him to pee. It was a good tip."

She shifted Gilbert so he could more easily drink from the bottle. "It sounds like Aunt Betty is a smart woman."

"She is. She's got a good heart, too. You don't find many like her anywhere you go."

"No, I reckon not."

He ventured another look her way, afraid she'd wonder why he couldn't seem to stop staring at her. She hadn't told him much about her life in Atlanta. He wanted to find out everything about her, especially why she willingly gave up all the comforts back home to spend the rest of her life with him. She had given up everything, and he was gaining everything. It didn't seem like a fair trade. Yet even after warning her, she insisted she wanted to come.

"I don't know what I did to deserve the good fortune of you coming all the way here to marry me," he began as he led the horses down a path that led directly to his home. "You're so beautiful. I can't help but think of all the disappointed suitors you left behind. I mean, you didn't mention any, but surely, you had men lined up in hopes of courting you."

"Oh," she replied, a slight hint of pink in her cheeks, "if I had any suitors, none of them were worth marrying."

"I know you took a big gamble in coming here. It couldn't have been an easy decision, even if the suitors weren't worth your time." Heat rose to his face as he contemplated saying more, but she was his wife now, and if he couldn't say it to her, then he couldn't say it to anyone. Clearing his throat, he added, "I'm the luckiest man in the world."

Her gaze went to Gilbert who was halfway through finishing his bottle.

He probably startled her with his words, but he hoped he did it in a good way. He didn't consider himself graceful with women when it came to romance but hopefully she wouldn't mind his meager attempts at wooing her.

His cabin came into view just beyond the final bend in the dusty path. He gestured to the small wooden structure nestled next to the side of the hill. In front was the well he'd dug when he first came out here. Not too far was his barn with a fenced-in area for the animals. He had only heard of the elegant houses on the plantations from people who had traveled by his parents' homestead in Minnesota. This was nothing like that.

Chancing another glance in her direction, he gauged her reaction to the place. She didn't seem as disheartened as he feared she'd be. Sure, he'd warned her in his first letter, but there was no way he could have adequately prepared her for it.

"I only have two bedrooms," he told her, though he'd already mentioned it. "I have some space for a loft, and I figure when we have more children, our bedroom will go up there. For the time being, we should be comfortable."

"The place suits me just fine, if that's what you're worried about," she assured him with that heartwarming smile of hers.

He loved her already. He barely knew a thing about her and everything happened so fast but he knew he loved her as much as he knew his own name. There were just some things that automatically happened to a person, and he assumed love was one of them.

He led the horses up to the front of the cabin and set the brake. "I'll get you and Gilbert down." Though it was probably unnecessary to tell her, he didn't want her to assume people this far removed from society didn't have manners. He jumped down from the wagon and hurried to her side. He waited for her to set the empty bottle on the floor of the wagon before he held his hand out to her. "Welcome home, Mrs. Grover."

"Thank you," she replied, her voice soft as she scooted to the edge of the seat.

One arm securely holding Gilbert, she accepted his hand and descended from the wagon. He took the opportunity to hold her for a moment, appreciating the way her curves pressed against him. He imagined it'd be wonderful to hold a woman in his arms, but this was much better than he expected.

Noting the way her cheeks grew pink, he released her. In his eagerness, he forgot to remember she wasn't accustomed to being near men in such a familiar fashion. "I'm sorry. I didn't mean to make you uncomfortable."

As he walked to the back of the wagon so he could start unloading it, she followed him, rubbing Gilbert's back. "You're my husband. You of all people have the right to be close to me."

He glanced at her, sensing the sincerity in her words. Relaxing, he said, "Living out here can get lonesome. I mean, I have Gilbert, and I know the people around here. But it's not the same as having a woman around. Not that I only wanted to get married for that reason. It's definitely to my benefit you are a woman. You're much better to look at than men are."

He cleared his throat. Somehow, what he wanted to say and what was coming out of his mouth were two different things, and for the life of him, he wasn't sure how to get the matter resolved.

"I'm glad that I am here," she said, saving him from inadvertently making more of a fool of himself. "I did come from a place with many people, but I never felt like I belonged there. With you, I have the chance to have a home."

Surprised, he turned from the large crate closest to him and faced her. "You weren't happy in Atlanta?"

She hesitated for a moment. "Did I sound like I was happy in my letter?"

"It's hard to tell whether or not someone is happy from a letter. I assumed you looked forward to something new since you assured me that you had nothing worth staying for. When I think about it, I suppose you didn't sound happy." He shrugged. "I guess money can't buy everything."

"No, it can't," she softly replied.

"I might not have money, but I promise I'll do everything I can to make you happy. This place might lack the finery you're used to," he gestured to his simple land and cabin, "but what it doesn't have in things, it makes up for in other ways. I'll be a good husband."

"I have no doubt about that. I just hope I can be a good wife."

"Oh, I know you will."

"You do?" she asked, her eyebrows furrowed.

"Of course. Just look at Gilbert. Aunt Betty says a baby has a sense about people. You can tell the heart of a person by the way a baby reacts to someone. I told you before, it's fate. We were meant to be together."

"Well, I'll do my best."

"I know you will." He gathered the crate and pulled it off the wagon. "Make yourself at home. I'll bring in the things we bought from the mercantile."

She nodded then turned to the house.

He couldn't help but notice the way she gently swung her hips from side to side as she walked. She had a lovely figure. And to boot, she was a beauty. He didn't know what he did to get so lucky, but he wouldn't question it. He'd just be glad that she happened to stumble upon his ad. There were some things he learned long ago not to question and fate was one of them. Whistling, he followed her into the house.

Chapter Three

Sadie stepped into the cabin and took a good look at the bare furnishings. A dining table with a couple chairs next to a worktable and cookstove, and a couple rocking chairs. Gilbert stirred in her arms but didn't wake up. Rubbing his back, she proceeded to one of the other two rooms.

The first was Gilbert's room since it had a crib and a small table with a wash basin and some cloth diapers with a pail nearby. A small box stove was against the wall. In the other room, she saw a bed, a dresser, a trunk, and a wash basin on a small nightstand. A box stove wasn't too far from the foot of the bed. She figured this far up north, it wasn't a bad idea to have as much heat in the rooms as possible.

Turning from what was going to be her bedroom, she looked up and saw the small loft that Al had mentioned. A ladder went up to it. She took a few steps back and tried to figure out what was up there, but it was too dark to tell.

Al came into the room and set the crate on the worktable. "I know this place needs a woman's touch. You can do whatever you want to it."

Her first thought was to say she couldn't come right in and change his home. In some ways, the bareness of it was refreshing after the gaudy red and purple furnishings and heavy drapes that had covered the brothel. But then she figured Hazel had come from excessive furnishings in her home and would jump at the chance to make the place more feminine. She, however, didn't have to be too feminine.

Perhaps if she chose softer colors like yellow or blue for decorating, Al wouldn't suspect she wasn't Hazel. She wondered if Hazel had shared some of her favorite colors with him. Probably not. Of all the things she'd mention to a man she was going to meet, she wouldn't think of colors.

Before Al left to get another crate, she asked, "What kind of things do you want me to do to your cabin?"

He paused on his way to the door and looked over at her and smiled. "I'll leave that up to you. I figure you know more about what a woman wants than I do. And besides, this is now your cabin, too."

Sensing the slight teasing tone in his voice, she chuckled "I'm not much into flashy or fancy things. I like to keep things simple."

"Simple works for me."

Relaxing, she returned his smile. "I'll see what I can do."

After he left the cabin, she went over to the shelf and hooks lining the wall and took note of the meager pots, pans and dishes. To the side were some bottles for Gilbert.

She loved how simple the entire cabin was. It spoke of an honest man who worked hard to provide for his son. And better yet, it didn't smell of perfume, alcohol, or sex.

But it did strike her as a bit odd that there was no indication a woman had ever lived here. She expected something feminine to linger around the place. A woman had to have given birth to Gilbert, after all. But then if they hadn't been married, she might not have lived here.

Gilbert stirred again in her arms and this time she became aware of a foul odor coming from his diaper. She bit her lower lip. Holding the child was one thing. Changing him was a completely different matter. She had absolutely no experience with babies. She had done good to feed him.

Al came in with the second crate, and she forced out, "How do you change a diaper?"

He set the crate on the table. "I'll show you."

Relieved he'd so easily accepted the task, she smiled her thanks as he took Gilbert from her. She followed him to Gilbert's bedroom and watched as he set him on the small table.

"It's easier on a person's back if he's on the table instead of the floor, but you can change him on the floor if you wish," Al said as he retrieved a new cloth diaper. "I fold these ahead of time so they're ready when I need them."

She nodded but concentrated on his movements while he went through the process of removing the boy's soiled diaper. She caught the smell of the poop and had to put her hand over her mouth so she didn't gag.

"Believe it or not, you'll get used to it," Al assured her as he wiped the boy's bottom clean. "I didn't think I would when I first did this, but now it doesn't even bother me."

She hoped that was true. In the past, no matter how hard she tried, she couldn't get past the horrible smell of liquor on men's breaths when they were on top of her. Pushing the reminder away, she focused on the process as Al tossed the soiled diaper and cloth towel into the pail full of ammonia then slipped the new diaper under his son. He slipped the pins in to secure it.

"You make it look easy," she commented, wondering how she'd ever be able to change a diaper so efficiently.

"It is once you get used to it. It'll take a few times doing it then you'll be a natural. I'm guessing it's easier for women to learn this kind of thing than it is for men. Women have a motherly instinct, after all."

Though she nodded her agreement, she wondered if that was true. Yes, she was a woman, but taking care of a baby wasn't something that seemed to come naturally to her. She'd been pregnant twice, but Madame's male friend beat her until she miscarried both times. It was the way all the prostitutes were treated at the brothel, and until now, it didn't occur to Sadie that she could have had a baby like Gilbert to care for. Not that a brothel was any place for a baby. And it wasn't like she had a choice anyway. She was Madame's property and Madame decided what happened to her.

"Hazel?"

A touch on her arm brought her attention back to Al. Her cheeks grew warm. She shouldn't have let her mind drift off to places where it shouldn't go. She was safe here. Safe with Al. And better yet, she was free. She never had to live under Madame's rules again.

"What do you need me to do?" she asked, knowing she missed whatever he'd said but not willing to tell him why.

"I asked if you'd take him out to the other room. I'm going to clean my hands." He gestured to the wash basin.

"Oh, of course."

She gathered Gilbert in her arms and left the small bedroom. Unsure of what to do, she decided to sit in one of the rocking chairs, thinking Gilbert might like to rest against her as he had before but he insisted on sitting up in her lap. He reached out for nothing in particular, and the action made her stop trying to rock him. For a little boy, he sure was strong. She had to wrap her arms around his waist so he didn't fall forward.

Al emerged from the bedroom and chuckled. "Now that he's had his nap, he'll want to move around."

Oh, so that's what Gilbert wanted. Sadie didn't know why she assumed the boy would be content to sit with her all day. That only showed how much she needed to learn about babies.

"It's a shame," she admitted as she placed the boy on the floor. "I enjoyed holding him."

"You have nothing to worry about. He'll love being held a couple hours after supper. He enjoys being rocked in that chair before bedtime."

Her gaze went to the boy who scooted across the floor to the worktable.

"I have one more crate to bring in," Al told her. "Then we'll put the things where you want them, and we'll work on supper."

Surprised, she asked, "Is it time for supper already?"

"Well, I usually have supper around six, but I thought you might want to eat early. You've had a long trip, and I figure you must be hungry."

He was right. Her stomach was growling. She cleared her throat. "I don't want to cause you any trouble." Especially after all he'd done for her already. "I can wait until six."

"Nonsense. It won't hurt me to eat early." He pointed to her hat and the drawstring purse hanging on her arm. "You can take those things off and make yourself at home."

With an uneasy laugh, she said, "I forgot I still had them with me. Where should I put them?"

"Anywhere you want, though I suggest putting them out of Gilbert's reach. He might not look like it, but he's quick and he'll drool all over your things if you let him."

He headed back out to the wagon and she glanced at the boy who was studying one of the legs of the worktable. The boy was so curious about his surroundings. Smiling, she removed her hat, the sweat causing her bun to be matted down. It was a relief to have it off.

Gilbert looked over at her as if seeing her for the first time.

Chuckling, she said, "I'm the same person as I was before. See?" She put the hat back on and he blinked. Taking it off, she decided to put it on the coat tree. "I suppose I do look quite a bit different without it. But you'll get used to it. I promise."

The boy smiled and she couldn't help but lose her heart to him. He was such a happy child. She supposed all babies were happy. But what surprised her was how a simple action could make her feel better.

She removed her gloves and went to what would now be her and Al's bedroom. She tried not to think about the bed or what it meant. After all the time she'd spent in bed with a man, she hadn't expected to be so nervous about what would be happening that night. But he wasn't paying her for a service. He wouldn't be running off as soon as he was done. She'd wake up tomorrow and he'd be next to her. From now on, she'd only share a bed with him.

Forcing her gaze off the bed, she went to the dresser and opened the drawers until she found three that were empty. She slipped her gloves in the top one. This would be a good place for small items. The other two would be for her clothes. There wasn't much space, but it was enough to suit her. In fact, she had more space now than she did at the brothel. She'd definitely improved her station in life by marrying Al.

Hazel, of course, would have been worse off, considering the wealth she'd left behind. Sadie examined her hands. While she didn't have any calluses on them, the nails were chipped and the skin dry from the times she'd washed them. She didn't have any lotion, but she did pick up beeswax, rose water and olive oil while at the mercantile. She knew how to mix the ingredients to heal her skin. She would have to make some lotion tomorrow.

As it was, the day was getting late and she was exhausted. What she wanted more than anything was to fall asleep and stay that way until morning, but she would tend to her wifely obligation first. Maybe Al would be satisfied with doing it one time. If that was the case, then she could get a good night's sleep. If he wasn't in the habit of visiting the brothel she'd seen as she entered town, then it wouldn't take him long to finish. She always preferred the customers who didn't frequent such establishments just because she knew they tended to be quicker and gentler. Madame might have loved the regulars since they brought in steady payments, but Sadie hated them. They had absolutely no respect for anyone.

She slammed the drawer shut.

"Are you alright?" Al called out from the other room.

"I'm fine," she replied before he came into the room to check on her. "I slipped."

She waited for the sound of footsteps but he only called out, "Alright. I'm going to put the wagon and horses in the barn."

When she heard the door close, she released her breath and wiped the tears from her eyes. Getting out of Nebraska was the best thing she ever did.

Once her nerves were settled, she went to the wash basin and lathered up the soap then washed her hands. She had a tendency to scrub them more than necessary, but it had become a habit over the years. Scrubbing her skin was the only way she didn't still feel grimy and disgusting after being with those men.

When she was done, she dried her hands on the towel and wondered if the past would always haunt her. She didn't know why she thought once she came to this small town that she wouldn't give a single thought to how her life had been. If anything, the stark contrast only made her more aware of where she came from.

Maybe she was a fool. Just what made her think she could successfully pull off this ruse? Sooner or later all things came to light and Al would find out the truth…wouldn't he?

No. There was no reason he had to know. Ever. She was miles and miles from Omaha. No one would find her. She was safe here. She could make a new start. She could be someone else. She'd be Mrs. Al Grover. No matter what it took, she'd do it. And if the memories of her past always haunted her, then so be it.

***

After Al finished tending to the animals, he returned to the house. The day had been a long one and he bet Hazel was hungry enough to eat anything he could make. If he didn't think it'd overwhelm her, he would have taken her to Aunt Betty's for a good meal, but she needed time to adjust to her new life. The least he could do was let her rest.

He smiled at her as he went over to the worktable which still had the boxes on them.

She stood up from the chair and walked over to him wiping her hands on her skirt. "I wasn't sure what you wanted me to do, and Gilbert was content to scoot around the floor. I thought I'd sit and wait for you to return."

"You don't have to wait for me in order to do anything. Do whatever you want," he replied.

Though she nodded, he sensed an uncertainty in her. It was on the tip of his tongue to ask her if she'd never been given any choices in her past. She hadn't said much about her life in Atlanta in her two letters, but he got the impression she was risking a lot to come out to marry him.

He suspected her parents hadn't been pleased to learn of her decision, and now that he saw how beautiful she was, she definitely could have done much better than him. But maybe she came here because it was the first time she had a choice. He'd heard that some women weren't given the freedom to do things they wanted to. Perhaps she'd been one of them.

Well, if that was the case, he wanted to make sure she understood that her needs were as important to him as his own. "Hazel," he began as he opened the first box, "I want you to know that you can do whatever you want around here. This is as much your home as it is mine, and you're my wife, not my servant. I want you to be happy here."

She smiled. "You're a good man, aren't you?"

That was a curious question, but it gave him some insight into what her life had been like. And that being the case, he got the impression that she hadn't been sad to leave her family. Deciding not to voice his observation, he left the box and closed the distance between them. He cupped her face in his hands and tilted her head up so her gaze met his.

Her eyebrows furrowed and her mouth turned down slightly in apprehension, as if she didn't know what to do.

Well, in time she would come to understand he meant what he said. In the meantime, he would show her. He brushed his thumb along her lips. "Can I kiss you?" he whispered.

She swallowed and offered a hesitant nod.

Closing his eyes, he lowered his head and kissed her. Given his limited experience with women, he hadn't known exactly what to expect, and she probably found him lacking because of that but he enjoyed it more than anything else he'd ever done. It was much better than the kiss they'd shared after their vows. Reluctantly, he ended it.

Al let out a slight chuckle. "You've probably had better kisses than that from your suitors back in Atlanta." The men there were probably a lot more charming, too.

Before she could respond, he turned his attention back to the boxes. "I better put these things away so we can get started on supper. Gilbert will want to eat before long, too. They say a woman runs the home, so I should put these where you want them." He pulled out a few items from one of the boxes and showed them to her. "Where do you want me to put these?"

"Oh...um..." She looked at the shelves. "I can reach those easily."

With a nod, he hurried to put them up for her. "I'll put in another shelf, one that is closer to your height. When I built this place, I had some help, but I didn't have a woman's help in figuring out where to put everything. I'm willing to make any changes you need, though. I realize it won't be anything fancy like what you're used to, but I can make it more comfortable than it is. Don't be afraid to let me know what you want."

She stared at him for a minute, as if she needed time to figure out the right thing to say. Finally, she walked over to the table, glanced at the contents in the boxes, and then turned her gaze to him. "You really are a good man."

Not sure why hearing her say that again should make him blush, he shrugged and took more items out of the box. "I only know how to be who I am. There's nothing much to me. Not really." After he put the items on the shelf, he went to another box and lifted the fabric and supplies for the clothes she'd make. "I'm not sure where you want these."

He held them out to her, and she took them. "Thank you," she said. "For everything."

"It's nothing. Besides, you need clothes. While what you have on right now looks good, Aunt Betty says a woman likes to have more than one dress to wear."

She let out a soft chuckle. "She's right."

"Well, I'll finish putting these things away while you take care of that. When you come back, I'll make supper."

"You're going to make supper?"

"You've had a long journey. I can't ask you to cook tonight. I can't promise it'll be as good as what you're used to, but I don't do too bad when it comes to fixing meals. And don't worry about Gilbert. I'll take care of him, too. I want you to rest, alright?"

She looked back at the soft material in her arms then smiled at him. "Alright."

He returned her smile in time for her to turn and head for their bedroom. Yes, he was already in love with her. And maybe in time, she would come to return his feelings.

Chapter Four

A couple hours later, Sadie's hands shook as she closed the door behind her. Collapsing against it, she pulled out the small bottle of olive oil from her pocket. If she wanted tonight to go as quickly as possible, she needed to be ready for him. And she didn't have much time. Al had just changed Gilbert's diaper and was feeding him for bedtime.

She couldn't get over the fact that he was a good man. She'd only heard of such men. Men who put others' needs ahead of their own. But until now, she'd never met one. And to think she was married to him. Hazel certainly knew how to pick a good one. And if anyone deserved a wedding night, it was him.

After she slipped out of her clothes and draped them over the back of the rocking chair, she twisted the lid off the bottle and poured a little of the liquid on her fingers before placing the oil inside her. It was a familiar routine and one she hated, but it was necessary if she didn't want to end up sore the next day.

When she was done making sure she was slick enough, she hid the bottle back in her dress pocket then crawled into the bed and pulled the thin blanket up to her chin. This was it. Soon Al would come into the room. She gulped and closed her eyes, willing herself to calm down. This wasn't how a newly married woman should be coming to her bed. Yes, she was supposed to be nervous. That was to be expected. But she wasn't supposed to be in absolute dread.

She took a deep breath, held it, then slowly released it. She'd done this before. Many times. She just needed to think of something else while he was doing it. But what? The blue or yellow dress she'd make? The breakfast she was going to attempt tomorrow morning? The buildings she'd seen in town? The long ride here?

Opening her eyes, she studied the small bedroom with the remaining sunlight that filtered through the open window. It wasn't much bigger than what she'd been used to, but there was no smell of perfume, sex or liquor in the room. That was a huge relief. She just might get through this without wanting to vomit afterwards.

Forcing her mind off the memories, she studied the quaint dresser and table beside it which contained the wash basin and pitcher. Next to the bed was a window with curtains made out of potato sacks. She frowned and took note of the quilt. It was frayed along the edges and had gray and blue squares.

She hadn't noticed how masculine the room was before. It was just like the rest of the small home now that she thought about it. What a strange thing. There was nothing feminine about the entire place, except for her. Maybe he hadn't been married to Gilbert's mother. Or maybe he was glad when she died and threw out all traces of her? There were so many questions she had and she couldn't ask any of them because he probably explained all of it to Hazel.

The door creaked open and she stiffened. In her curiosity, she'd forgotten what was about to take place. Clutching the blanket to her chin, she looked over at Al who set the kerosene lamp on the dresser.

"Do you want me to turn the light off?" he asked.

"No. Please leave it on."

"Are you sure?"

She nodded. The light made it easier to focus on something—anything—in the room.

"How much do you want me to dim it?" he asked.

"What you have right now is fine."

"It's pretty bright."

"I don't mind it being bright."

"Alright." He left the dresser and pulled the potato sack curtain shut. Then he glanced her way. "I don't know if you want to watch me undress or not, but I wanted to warn you in case you wanted to shut your eyes or something."

Despite the awkward position she was in, a smile tugged at her lips. "I'll just stay here and wait for you."

That was simple enough. She'd done it often enough in the past. The men hadn't warned her they were going to remove their clothes—and some only dropped their pants low enough to get to it. But he was a gentleman. She knew it as soon as he warned her that he was going to undress. He'd never step foot inside a godforsaken brothel.

She closed her eyes and swallowed. Hazel was a virgin. She had to play the part of one if she didn't want him to figure out she was more experienced than a woman had the right to be. She could hear him removing his clothes and her mind went back to her old bedroom where she'd waited on her bed, fighting the urge to either cry or scream.

Her eyes flew open and she stared at the ceiling. This wasn't her old room. It was her new one. And in this one, only her husband would be touching her and kissing her. It was still a transaction. But it was different from the kind it had been with the men in her past. For them, it was sexual gratification for money. In this case, she'd offer him her body for pleasure, but he'd given her his name, his home, and his protection. At least in this situation, she was getting things she wanted.

A movement from the corner of her eye caught her attention and she turned her head, her heart threatening to stop when she saw that he wasn't wearing anything. She swallowed the bile that rose up in her throat and looked at the drapes.

The bed shifted under his weight as he slipped in next to her. The bed was much too small. She could feel his bare flesh pressing against hers, his erection indicating his excitement over what was about to happen. She took a deep breath to steady her nerves. She could do this. She *had* to do this.

"Hazel," he whispered, his voice gentle as he caressed her cheek.

He expected her to make eye contact with him. She was going to have to oblige him because that's what Hazel would do. She forced her gaze to meet his, noting his thick lashes.

"I know this is your first time, and I'm going to try to be as gentle as possible," he said. "If you don't like anything, let me know and I'll stop. Alright?"

Making herself nod, she managed a stiff, "Alright."

He lowered his head and kissed her, something that surprised her since she fully expected him to reach for her breast right away. His lips were soft and hesitant. Raising his head, he took another good look at her, his eyes searching hers. "Do you want to wait?"

"No," she quickly replied. If he didn't do it tonight, she'd have to go through the next day in dread of this. At least if they did it now, he should be good for a few days. Then she could relax and settle into this life. "I…I'm just nervous, since this is my," she tried not to wince, "first time and all."

The lie was harder to say than she thought it'd be, but it worked. He relaxed and offered her a smile. "I'm really glad you left Atlanta to come here. I know in my ad I said I was looking for a mother for Gilbert, but the truth is, I also wanted a wife, someone who would be a friend and lover." He chuckled. "I didn't want to come out and say I was lonely. It doesn't seem like the kind of thing a man admits."

She cleared her throat and returned his smile. "I was lonely, too."

"Even with all the extravagant balls and men vying for your hand?"

Was that what Hazel's life had been like? Going from one dance to another, holding hopeful suitors at bay? "None of those men meant anything to me," she finally replied, figuring it best to let him think what he wanted even as she told him the truth.

"Well, I'm honored and forever grateful you came all the way out here to marry me. I promise I'll do everything I can to make you glad you made the sacrifice."

He saved her from having to reply because he kissed her again. This time she responded to him, knowing if she didn't, he would probably stop, and as much as she'd like him to tell her more about himself and what he and Hazel wrote to each other, there was still the pressing matter of the wedding night to resolve first.

He brought her into his arms and held her as he deepened the kiss. Had it not been for his arousal which rested against her abdomen, she might have enjoyed it. But she did her best to act as if she did, and he must have believed it since he didn't stop.

Before long, he pursued a more intimate exploration of her body, the light providing more than enough opportunity to do so. He traced her breasts with his hands before he brought his mouth to her nipples to tease them. Though he was gentle, taking great care in touching her, she wasn't really aware of what he was doing.

She let out moans when appropriate, as she'd been taught, but she focused on the drapes, noting the hints of a cobweb lining the top of them on the right side of the window. She didn't know if she should remove the cobweb or not. It proved to be a good focal point during this act, and she knew this wouldn't be the only time he'd want to do it.

Suddenly, his mouth was on her neck, his breathing heavy as his body wiggled between her legs. She gulped and gripped the pillow under her head. This was it. Soon—very soon—it'd be over. At least he wasn't one of those men who felt the need to prove himself by trying to get her to climax. Like she could ever truly enjoy herself while doing this!

He lifted his head. "Hazel?"

It took her a moment to realize he was talking to her. And this forced her to look at him instead of focusing on the drapes. She caught the worried expression on his face and knew she was doing a horrible job of pretending to be the woman he expected to share his bed with tonight. "I'm sorry. I'm just…nervous, you know?"

"Maybe we should wait."

She stopped him before he could get off of her. "No!" Recalling Gilbert who was sleeping in the other room, she lowered her voice. "I want to do this." To get it over with. "Please? It'll be worse if we wait."

He winced. "Worse?"

"I meant, my nervousness will get worse."

"I don't know. I want this to be something you'll enjoy."

Then he'd be waiting forever because she'd never enjoy it, no matter how tender he was. And he was amazingly tender. Whatever connection he and Hazel made through their correspondence, he obviously cared about her.

"Something about this doesn't feel right," he said then got off of her. "I'm sorry, but I can't do it. Not when it feels like I'm forcing you to do it."

She sat up in the bed as he went to retrieve his underwear. "You're not forcing me. I came here willingly."

He slipped on his underwear and shook his head. "I know, but it's not right."

She stared at him, not believing her ears. Did he suspect she wasn't really Hazel?

"I'm sorry, Hazel. I don't want to make you more nervous than you already are, but maybe things will be better after we get to know each other." He pulled open a drawer and pulled out one of his shirts. "Would you like something to wear?"

Realizing he really wasn't going to follow through with the ordeal, she decided she'd better take the shirt.

He handed it to her before he turned down the wick on the kerosene lamp. Glancing her way, he asked, "Do you need some light to sleep?"

"Some, if you don't mind." Unable to look at him anymore, she buttoned the shirt, aware of the masculine scent associated with it.

When he settled back into the bed, he turned toward her. "Is it alright if I hold you?"

What a strange thing for a man to ask. He refused to consummate the marriage, but thought he could just hold her? She'd been around men. Once they touched a woman, they had to do everything else. So maybe she could get this whole thing over with after all. Relieved, she said, "Of course, you can hold me."

He wrapped his arms around her and drew her into his embrace. He was stronger than most men, probably because he worked with his hands. Out here in the wilderness, he had to rely on his physical strength to support himself and his son. Now, he would be supporting her, too. From what she'd seen, he didn't have much to his name, and she could understand why he wondered if Hazel could accept this new change. Hazel had been used to a privileged lifestyle, one with fancy gowns, servants, and other things money could buy.

Sadie thought back to her initial meeting with Hazel. Hazel had been wearing a beautiful dark blue dress, but it wasn't the dress that initially caught her attention. She had been huddled in the corner of a restaurant, seeming as if she needed to get away from someone or something. That was what caught Sadie's attention. She recognized a desperate plight when she saw one. It was how she felt every day of her life. And she couldn't resist trying to rescue Hazel from whatever it was she was hiding from.

"Do you need help?" Sadie had asked as she approached the small table.

Sadie lifted the veil from her hat so the woman could see her face. When in public, Sadie didn't dare reveal her true identity in case it brought shame to Madame Eleanor's business. Prostitutes, after all, were to be discrete when entertaining men in the community who didn't want to tarnish their reputation by being seen entering a brothel. In that case, Madame arranged a private meeting in a place of their choosing and dressed the prostitute in ladylike attire with a veil to conceal her identity, lest another man who didn't mind frequenting a brothel recognize her and expose the secret rendezvous. Only prostitutes Madame trusted not to run off were allowed to go to such meetings, and Sadie welcomed the chance to get out into polite society, if even for an hour.

Now, as she watched Hazel wipe the tears from her eyes with a lace handkerchief, Sadie felt a pull to go to the woman and help her, to make sure she never ended up in a situation Sadie had been forced into. Hazel looked much too fragile to handle such a hardship.

"Do you need help?" Sadie repeated, this time using a louder voice among the talk going on around them.

Hazel looked up at her and then scanned the room.

Sadie quickly put down her veil and glanced behind her but didn't see anyone who seemed interested in them. She turned back to Hazel and lifted the veil. "Do you need money? I can give you some."

The restaurant owner had just paid her for her services and had left a significant tip, one in which she had planned to hide from Madame but could give to this poor woman who had an innocence about her.

Hazel shook her head. "No."

Sadie waited for a moment, quickly debating her options. She could leave and never see Hazel again, but somehow that didn't seem right. Though Hazel hadn't extended the invitation, she sat across from her and leaned forward, careful to keep her voice low so none of the other patrons would overhear her. "You're not from here. I can tell that from your Southern accent. I don't mean to pry in your business, but you have no male companion and seem scared. Those are two things that could get you caught up in something you don't want to be in." Like a brothel, but she didn't dare add that. The poor thing was frightened enough as it was.

"I know." She wiped more tears away. "I'm trying to get to a young man who posted a mail-order bride ad. I have to get there."

"I don't understand," Sadie whispered. "You said you have money. What's stopping you from getting there?"

Hazel opened her mouth to speak but then she coughed, and one cough led to another and another. People started turning their attention to stare at them. Mindful of Madame, Sadie quickly covered her face with the veil. Rising to her feet, she asked for a glass of water and a man sitting at a nearby table handed her one.

She gave it to Hazel. "Here, drink this. It should help."

Hazel tried to take a sip but couldn't stop coughing long enough to swallow any water. She placed the handkerchief up to her mouth and when she lowered it, Sadie saw the blood on the cloth.

Alarmed, she ran over to Hazel and called out for someone to get a doctor.

Chapter Five

"Doctor… Someone get a doctor…"

Al stirred as his wife murmured for a doctor in her sleep. It took him a moment to wake up and realize she was only dreaming. He turned toward her and studied her in the morning light that filtered through the slit in the drapes and landed across her forehead. She had left his arms at some point in the middle of the night and was curled up on her side, hugging her legs and furrowing her eyebrows.

Leaning over her, he smiled and brushed aside a strand of auburn hair that fell across her eyes. Her hair was slightly messed up from her night's sleep, but it in no way detracted from her appeal. He couldn't help but recall the rest of her. Generous soft breasts, narrow waist, the auburn curls that hid her most secret place. He shifted to relieve the pressure of his arousal. Last night hadn't gone the way he'd hoped, but he could in no way blame her. She hadn't known a man before, and they'd only met yesterday. Even if she was afraid she'd get more nervous because he'd decided to wait, deep down, he knew this was for the best. It was what she needed.

"Doctor," she whispered.

What could she be dreaming about? In his brief correspondence with her, there was no mention of a doctor. She said she'd grown up on a plantation and that her father was well-to-do. Her mother died a couple years earlier, and she said that was why his ad appealed to her. She wanted to come out and be Gilbert's mother. Maybe as Hazel slept, she was thinking of the time the doctor came to visit her ailing mother.

Maybe seeing Gilbert brought back those memories and how much she wanted to fill in the gap she said a child would have if he didn't have the kind of nurturing only a mother could give him. She'd warned him that she didn't know the first thing about caring for babies, but she also assured him that she was more than happy to learn. He smiled. He had no doubt that she'd be a wonderful mother.

"Someone get the doctor," she whispered again, taking Al's attention off the letters she'd written him.

She opened her eyes. For a moment, she stared ahead of her as if not really seeing anything, and then she blinked and looked around the room. When her gaze finally turned in his direction, he smiled and brushed her cheek with his thumb. "Good morning."

She offered a small smile in return. "Morning."

Lowering his head, he gave her a soft kiss, and she stiffened slightly. "Did I do something wrong?" he asked, pulling away from her so he could get a better look at her face.

For a moment she seemed to have the same look in her eyes that a startled deer got when he went hunting, and it made him wonder even more about her past. Did men easily startle her or was it because she still wasn't sure about him in particular? He reached forward and caressed her cheek. She didn't seem to mind it so much if he gently touched her, and if he was right, she relaxed.

"I hope you'll come to understand that you have nothing to fear with me," he whispered.

"I know."

Though she said those words, he wondered if she truly did understand it. But if she didn't, was there anything he could say to make her? In this case, all he could do was show her through his actions. Hopefully in time, she would realize he was telling her the truth.

"It's about time for Gilbert to wake up," he said as he rose up from the bed.

"You don't want to…to finish what you started last night?" she asked.

Of course he did, but one look at her was all he needed to know it wasn't the right time. Not when it was apparent she wasn't ready. "There's no need to rush it. We have the rest of our lives to do it." Then, in an effort to lighten the mood, he took out his razor and asked, "Do you prefer men who have a mustache, a beard, or shave everything off?"

As he hoped, her smile returned and there was a hint of mirth in her eyes. "What do you care what I prefer?"

"I never have to look at myself, but you'll be stuck looking at me all the time. The least I can do is present myself in a way that's suitable to you. So, what would you like me to do?"

"Since you asked, I like a man who shaves it all off."

"You do?"

"Yes. I like seeing the whole face."

"Then I shall do your bidding, my lady."

He bowed and she giggled. With a grin, he turned his attention to shaving his face while she got dressed in the same clothes she had on the day before. From time to time, his gaze left the mirror in front of him so he could steal a glance at her, very much intrigued by the soft curves of her body. Even though he'd explored all of her the previous night, he didn't think he'd ever get tired of seeing her without clothes on. She was much better looking without them on.

Once she was done, she cleared her throat and turned to face him. "What would you like to eat for breakfast?"

"Believe it or not, I make pancakes and bacon on most days."

"You do?"

He set down his razor and washed his face. "Surprised?"

"Well…yes. I didn't think men cooked."

"It depends on the man. I do a lot of hunting and have learned to make some pretty tasty meals, if I do say so myself. Perhaps you'd like to sample a steak tonight?"

"You eat steak? But doesn't that get expensive?"

"Not when I get it myself. One nice thing about living out here is that there's plenty of animals to hunt. The hardest part is cutting up the meat."

"I've never done anything like that."

"I didn't think the daughter of a wealthy land owner would."

She turned her gaze from him and brushed her hair.

After he dressed for the day, he parted the drapes to let the sunlight in the room. Doing so permitted the light to touch the silky waves in Hazel's hair as she was brushing it, accentuating the auburn highlights in it.

"It's a shame you have to pull your hair back into a bun," he said as he approached her.

She turned her head in his direction and he took in the lovely sight of her. With her long hair resting softly over her shoulders and the sunlight framing a halo around her head, she was the most beautiful woman he'd ever seen.

"I've never seen a more breathtaking sight than you." He reached out to touch her hair, marveling at how soft the strands were. "You'll think it's silly," he added with a chuckle, "but you look like an angel. Not that I've seen an angel, but if I did, I imagine one would look just like you."

Clearing her throat, she put the brush on the table and shook her head. "I'm not an angel, Al."

"Oh, I know. None of us are. Like I said, it was silly." He kissed her cheek. "I better get Gilbert up."

"Do you want me to do that? I am the woman after all. Women are supposed to take care of children."

"You just came here yesterday. You should take a couple days to rest. Take your time in getting ready."

"You're going to spoil me."

He smiled. "Just wait until you do laundry. You won't be thinking that then."

Her lips turned up at his joke and he left the room to take care of Gilbert.

***

Later that morning, Sadie watched Al through the window as he chopped wood in the front yard. She didn't understand it. He should have taken her up on her offer to enjoy intimate relations that morning. He hadn't completed the act last night, and when she woke up, he'd been fully erect. So why did he insist on rejecting her offer? Didn't all men want a woman, especially one who was willing to satisfy his needs?

With a shake of her head, she turned her attention back to Gilbert who was rocking back and forth in the rocking chair. He was chewing on a rattle and laughing. Curious, she scanned the room to see what was amusing him but didn't see anything remotely funny. Even so, his giggling was infectious and she found herself chuckling.

"You're a real wonder, aren't you?" she whispered.

She had no idea just how innocent babies were. She'd been like that once, too. Laughing and smiling because the world was brand new and full of many happy moments.

"I hope you're always this happy, Gilbert."

He looked her way, his large brown eyes focused on her.

She went over to him and knelt in front of him. She cupped his face in her hands, her smile growing wider despite the tears forming in her eyes. "I'm going to do everything I can to make sure you never discover how unkind this world can be. I want you to keep laughing."

He babbled and touched her cheeks as if to wipe her tears away.

She picked him up and held him. After a while, she sat down and rocked in the chair, hoping he'd remain still and let her enjoy this moment. She had no idea holding a baby was so wonderful, but it was quickly becoming her favorite thing to do.

"You're a lucky boy," she told him as he settled against her breast. "Your father's a good man. I didn't think men like him existed. He could have used me, like other men. But he didn't. Hazel couldn't have picked someone better."

And that only went to prove how smart Hazel had been. Whatever she'd been running from, she had chosen the right place to go to.

Resting her cheek against the top of Gilbert's head, she whispered, "I'm sorry you didn't make it, Hazel. But I'm glad you gave me a second chance."

She closed her eyes, recalling the doctor's bad news...

"I'm afraid she's not going to make it," he said as he washed his hands in the basin by the bed where Hazel slept.

"What's wrong with her?" Sadie whispered, her veil still covering her face.

The doctor turned to her and shrugged. "She has pneumonia. I'm surprised she managed to walk into the restaurant."

She watched as he placed a cool cloth on her forehead. Hazel winced but didn't wake up, which was good since she didn't have to go through any pain when she was sleeping. Sadie glanced at the bottles full of medicine lining the shelves and turned her attention back to the doctor. "Are you sure there's nothing here that can help her? I know someone who had pneumonia and survived."

"Her fever's too high."

"But that doesn't mean anything. People beat the odds all the time when someone says something is hopeless."

With a heavy sigh, he shook his head. "I'm sorry, ma'am. I know you don't want to see your friend die, but the outcome isn't always good for my patients." He picked up Hazel's purse and handed it to her. "Whatever affairs you need to get in order, I suggest you do so quickly. I don't think she'll make it through the night." After a moment, he squeezed her hands. "I'm sorry. I wish I could give you better news." He glanced at Hazel. "I need to pay another patient a visit. I won't be longer than a half hour."

Sadie nodded as he left the small building. Unsure of what else to do, she sat in the chair beside the bed and lifted her veil. The doctor would recognize her if he saw her face. But it wasn't because he'd been at the brothel to enjoy the pleasures of the flesh. It'd been because he had tended to her twice—both times after she miscarried. She didn't think he'd tell Madame Eleanor that she was there, but she didn't dare take her chances.

Her gaze lowered to the purse in her hands. Biting her lower lip, she fought the urge to tug at the strings and find out about the woman resting in front of her. It was hard to avoid temptation but she managed to do it.

Focusing on the sick woman, she touched her hand. "You'll think it's silly, but I heard that a kind touch and word can do wonders when someone isn't feeling well. So I thought I might as well talk to you. I don't know if you remember me, but I was the woman at the restaurant who sat at your table. My name is Sadie. Sadie Miller. Um… You know, you shouldn't pay the doctor any mind. He means well, of course, but miracles happen and you just might recover. Don't give up. You just keep holding on. As long as you got the will to live, you can do it."

Sadie blinked back her tears, her thoughts of the past drifting back to the corners of her mind as she heard the front door open. Her gaze went to Al who carried some split logs into the house.

"I wanted to get some wood ready," he explained as he set a couple by the cookstove. "I put most of them against the house. Before long, we'll need most of them."

"I suppose that's to be expected this far up north." Nebraska had its share of cold winters, too, but of course she couldn't tell him that.

Gilbert stirred in her lap and held his arms out to Al who walked over to him and picked him up. "How have things been between you two?" Al asked her.

"Good. He's a very easygoing baby," she replied. "He smiles and laughs all the time."

"Aunt Betty says he's one of the easiest babies she's ever come across."

Had she known anything about babies, she might have agreed with this woman. But there was no denying he was a very happy child. "I think the fact that he's an easy baby has something to do with the way you treat him."

"You think so?" he asked, bouncing the boy in his arms.

"Yes." Then, in a lower voice, she added, "I can tell you're a good man." She'd certainly been around enough bad ones to know the difference. Clearing her throat, she rose from the chair. "I should probably take that recipe book and learn how to make something."

"Are you sure you're up to it? You had a long journey out here. I'd think you'd still be tired."

"Aren't you tired? You spent all morning chopping wood after making breakfast."

He shrugged. "I'm used to doing everything for me and Gilbert."

She frowned, wondering just how long his first wife had been dead. From the sound of it, it'd been quite a while. Maybe she died in childbirth. She'd heard of it happening. And out here where there wasn't a doctor, it might be an even stronger possibility.

"Did I upset you?" Al asked, bringing her attention back to him.

"No."

He relaxed. "Good. You frowned and I thought I said something wrong. You'll have to forgive me. I'm not used to this kind of thing."

"This kind of thing?"

"You know," he motioned between them, "this whole husband and wife thing."

"Oh?"

Then maybe he hadn't been married. Maybe Gilbert was conceived and born out of wedlock. If that was the case, his mother could have likely died. Or maybe she ran off after he was born. How she wished Hazel had lived long enough to tell her more about him! She had so many questions and couldn't ask any of them.

Forcing the irritation aside, she smiled at Al and gestured to the cookstove. "I'm rested enough. Besides, the sooner I learn how to cook, the better."

"Alright." He set Gilbert on the floor and handed him a toy. "I don't expect him to actually play with it the whole time, but at least it'll keep him busy for a little bit."

She couldn't help but smile as he ruffled the boy's hair. The boy giggled then turned his attention to the toy.

Al joined her at the worktable. "He brings a lot of joy to my home. And now that you're here, it's even better." He leaned forward and gave her a kiss so soft she almost missed it. His face turned red and he cleared his throat. "I was thinking we could have country fried steak, beans, and biscuits tonight."

"That sounds wonderful."

"I'll be right back with it then."

"Al," she called out as he headed for the door.

He stopped and faced her. "Yes?"

"You don't ever have to feel shy about kissing me. I enjoyed it."

And it was true. When he kissed her, it was gentle and kind, so much like him. It wasn't sloppy or wet or slimy. He was nothing like those men had been, and she appreciated that most about him.

He cleared his throat again and offered a shy smile before he left the house.

Chapter Six

That night Sadie removed her clothes once more and slipped into bed. Again, she used oil to make it easy for him if he wanted to engage in intimate relations. She wasn't sure he'd want to be with her since he hadn't the night before. Well, that wasn't true. He had wanted to be with her. He just held back. She didn't understand why. No man had ever held back before. But for some reason he had, and she knew it had something to do with his feelings for her. He cared about her. He didn't see her as someone to use at his convenience.

So this was what being a wife was like. A wife was a person, someone cherished and protected. And she was in Al's home where he provided her with food, shelter and clothing. Her mind went to the fabrics he'd bought her at the mercantile. She'd have to get started on the dress tomorrow. She could do simple designs. It wouldn't be anything fancy. Maybe the woman he mentioned—Aunt Betty—would be able to teach her how to do a shirtwaist and skirt. What she'd make would look like a potato sack. She sighed. Maybe she should wait until she met Aunt Betty before attempting to sew anything.

Al came into the room and her attention went to him. This time she wasn't quite so nervous. She knew him better now—had a better understanding of who he was. She still couldn't watch him as he removed almost all of his clothing before he turned off the light in the kerosene lamp.

"Could you please leave a little light on?" she asked, hoping he didn't detect the unease in her voice as she scanned the darkness.

"No, I don't mind."

She waited until the dim light lit up the room before she released her breath. Good. Now in case he wanted to consummate the marriage, she could focus on something to take her mind off of what he would do to her. As he got into the bed, she studied his expression. "Do you think I'm difficult to be with?"

His gaze met hers. "No. Why would you think that?"

She shrugged. Madame had often said any woman who dared tell a gentleman what to do deserved whatever she got for being difficult. And sometimes 'whatever she got' involved bruises or rape. Both things equally unpleasant. Both things that haunted her when she thought back on them.

Al shifted on the bed and brushed back a tear that had fallen down her cheek. "What was your life like in Atlanta? Were your parents mean to you?"

Forcing back the other tears, she shook her head. "I don't want to talk about it." Who knew what Hazel's life had been like? It'd do no good to even make up something about it. Besides, that didn't seem fair to her memory. "I'm sorry, Al. I just want to focus on what we have."

He didn't answer right away, and that worried her. But then he brought her into his arms and encouraged her to settle her head on his shoulder. "Alright."

She frowned. Surely, it couldn't be that easy. "Alright?"

"I can't make you tell me anything you don't want to. The important thing is, you weren't married in Atlanta."

"No, I've never been married."

He kissed the top of her head. "Good. I wouldn't want some man trying to steal you from me."

Noting the teasing tone in his voice, she chuckled. She didn't know how he could make her feel better as easily as he did, but it was starting to occur to her that he could find a way to make her feel better, no matter what.

"If you ever want to tell me about Atlanta, I'd like to hear it, even if it's not pretty," he whispered. "I know life isn't always pretty."

Whatever bad things Hazel might have been through, there was no way it was worse than Sadie's past. And Hazel must have understood that since she insisted Sadie marry Al.

"Would you like to meet Aunt Betty next week?" he asked.

Glad for the change of topic, she nodded. "I'd be nice to meet someone who can help me sew and cook."

"She'll do that, but she might also talk your ear off. The woman has the gift of gab."

"Does she?"

"Yes. And she says she can tell if a person is good or not."

Sadie didn't like the sound of this. And since she'd already expressed an interest in seeing the woman, she couldn't very well go back and say she changed her mind, not without arousing his suspicions. She swallowed then forced out, "She can?"

"She can't tell anyone's past, of course. But she says she gets a feeling about people. Says it's something she just knows when she meets them."

"Oh."

"You have nothing to worry about. I already know you're a good woman."

She was anything but good, but she decided not to correct him.

"I hope I didn't just make you nervous. She doesn't pry into people's business. She won't try to get you to tell her about Atlanta."

"I'm looking forward to meeting her," she forced out.

"I can't wait for her to meet you. I was so excited when I got your reply, I went straight over to her and told her that my bride would be coming in September."

She couldn't help the smile that curled her lips upward. Never in her life had she met anyone more transparent in their feelings. It was refreshing in a world of manipulation. With Al, what people saw was what they got. He didn't play games nor was he distrusting of others. In many ways, he was like Gilbert...seeing the world through hope and embracing each moment with enthusiasm.

She closed her eyes and decided to enjoy this moment—this one sliver of time where it was just the two of them. A husband and wife sharing a contented experience. For years, she'd wondered what it was like to be a wife. And now she knew. It was a very sweet thing.

After a few minutes passed, she dared to brush her hand over his chest, thinking it might initiate lovemaking. He'd waited all through last night and today. Surely, he was anxious to consummate their marriage. A man, after all, had needs that demanded a woman's attention. Maybe tonight they could get it over with. Then she wouldn't have to keep waiting and wondering when he'd approach her for it.

When he didn't respond to her touch, she lifted her head and was surprised to discover that he'd fallen asleep. She furrowed her eyebrows. She was naked. Surely, he felt her breasts and bare legs. Didn't he want to do something about it?

But his chest rose up and down in a slow, steady rhythm that notified her that he was in deep sleep and would be so for quite some time. She lowered her head back on his chest and relaxed. Well, at least for tonight she was spared having to act like she enjoyed something she didn't.

It'd been a nice day. She'd managed to change a diaper all on her own. She'd taken a bath after Al filled up her tub with hot water and left her alone in this room. She'd assisted Al with breakfast and supper. She'd fed Gilbert and held him while rocking in the chair.

And just now, she'd shared a nice conversation with him. It'd been the perfect ending to a perfect day. She didn't think it was possible for a man to take such an interest in a woman without the pretense of getting into bed with her, but Al was proof that such men existed.

She smiled. Life here would be wonderful. Absolutely and completely wonderful.

***

Al shifted in his bed before dawn, aware that a warm body pressed intimately against him. He didn't have to open his eyes to know he wasn't dreaming. This was real. His arm was around Hazel's shoulders, and she was fast asleep. Yesterday had, no doubt, taken its toll on her. She was still recovering from her long journey up here. He didn't know how long it took her to get here from Atlanta, but he knew it was a tiring experience.

As much as he wanted to stay right there in bed with her, his arousal notified him that there was no way he could stay there. He hadn't done anything to take care of himself on their wedding night after it became clear that the timing was wrong. And the timing was still wrong. Something wasn't right, and though he'd tried to get her to tell him what it was, thinking that perhaps it had something to do with Atlanta, she wasn't telling him.

She needed more time. That was all he knew. And he'd wait for her. But in the meantime, he wasn't exactly a saint. He couldn't go without doing something. She most likely would be upset if she knew what he needed to do to relieve the pressure building up inside of him. She had offered to be intimate with him, after all. She'd wonder why he refused her offer and then took care of his own needs. And he didn't know if he could explain it to her so she'd understand.

The best time to do something was while she was still asleep. Then she wouldn't know, and he could go through the day without the ache getting worse.

He got out of the bed and put on his pants, careful not to wake her. Then he left the bedroom. The house was quiet and dark. Only the stream of moonlight coming in through the window lit the place up. He went outside. The air was chilly, but he was so aroused that he hardly noticed. He made sure he was far enough from the house, so he wouldn't be seen in case Hazel woke up and searched for him, before he sat on the ground. It wasn't the most comfortable spot around, but it afforded him privacy and that's what mattered.

He unbuttoned his pants and slid his hand over his erection. It wasn't going to take long for him to find his release. He already knew it, especially since he'd come so close to making love to Hazel the other night. Even now, he could vividly recall the soft curve of her breasts, the taste of her nipples as he ran his tongue along them, and the way he'd felt against her patch of curls as he got ready to enter her.

With a low moan, he grasped his aching member and stroked it in the rhythm that would guarantee his pleasure. It was heavenly to think of her, to remember his exploration of her in the soft glow of the kerosene lamp. One day they would be together again, and when they did, it would be right. She would feel loved and cared for. She wouldn't be doing it because it was her wifely duty or because she was afraid of doing it for the first time and just wanted to get it over with. When they finally came together, it would be because she loved him.

He moaned again and released his seed onto the ground. Out of breath, he waited for a couple minutes until his head cleared. No doubt, it would feel better when he was with her, but this would serve his purpose for the time being. It would buy him patience so he could sleep in the same bed with her and hold her in his arms.

He didn't want to give up holding her. That was one of his favorite parts of going to bed each night. It gave him something to look forward to, especially when the chores around the place became tedious. And it certainly was nice to kiss her. Everything about her was so lovely.

Noting the chill in the air, he buttoned his pants and rose to his feet. He returned to the cabin and made sure Gilbert was still asleep before he went to his bedroom. Hazel was curled up on her side, looking peaceful as she slept. He studied her for a moment. What would compel a woman so beautiful and pleasant to answer a mail-order bride ad? He couldn't believe that she didn't have men lined up to court her. Maybe someday she'd be comfortable enough to tell him.

He removed his pants and went to the bed. He didn't think about how cool his skin was until he brought her into his arms and realized how warm she was. After a moment, he was assured he hadn't woken her up and relaxed. Good.

Soon it would be time to wake up. But until then, he could go back to sleep and enjoy this time when he could hold her before the day's demands forced him away from her. He leaned forward and kissed her cheek. Then he settled his head on his pillow and closed his eyes. Within minutes, he drifted off to sleep.

Chapter Seven

A week later, Sadie pricked her finger on the needle and rubbed the sore spot with her thumb. It'd taken her a good fifteen minutes to put the thread through the tiny eye, and now it was proving to be a difficult task to work on the dress. The blue was such a nice color, too. It was the color of the sky, and she loved to look at the sky since she'd seen so much of it on the way to meet Al. It wasn't red or purple or gray. Those colors were the worst. They made her feel trapped.

But the light blue was wonderful. Now that she had met Al and realized what a kind person he was, she could associate this color with hope, peace, and joy. For the first time since her mother sold her to Madame, she was happy.

Swallowing the lump in her throat, she lowered the fabric and glanced at Gilbert who was scooting across the floor. It did her no good to think of her mother. Instead, she determined she would be a better mother. She would never sell Gilbert. If Al died and they had no money or place to stay, she'd go out and do whatever she had to in order to make sure he had something to eat. And if she couldn't... Well, she'd stay with him and, depressing as it would be, she'd die with him. There was no way she'd ever abandon him.

The front door opened so she turned her head in time to see Al come into the cabin with a rifle. "I caught sight of an elk not far from here. I'm going to see if I can get him. If I can, we'll be in good shape this winter."

Recalling the amount of food he had saved in his cellar, she thought he had enough already, but she certainly couldn't fault him for wanting extra—just in case.

"Will you be alright with Gilbert?" he asked.

"I'll be fine," she assured him.

"I hope I won't be too long, but sometimes it's hard to tell. If I come back with it, I'll show you how I cut up and preserve the meat."

Though the task didn't appeal to her at all, she realized she might have to do this chore in the future...or at least help him with it. "Alright."

"Good luck on the dress."

She smiled as he closed the door.

With another glance at Gilbert, she saw that he was content and turned her attention back to sewing. As she continued to pull the thread through the fabric, her mind drifted off to Hazel and that fateful day that made Sadie decide to come to Rapid City...

The woman moaned and Sadie leaned forward.

"Miss?" Sadie whispered, pressing her hand against the woman's cheek. She still had a fever and if Sadie was right, it was worse.

The woman grimaced and murmured something about water, so Sadie jumped up to pour her a glass.

"Here. Drink this." She brought the woman's head up so she could sip the cool liquid.

The woman started coughing and Sadie hurried to retrieve a clean cloth by the bed. As she feared, there was blood—more so than before. This wasn't good. It couldn't be good. Maybe she was just a prostitute, but the fact that the woman's condition was getting worse didn't bode well.

"Hold on, Miss," Sadie encouraged as she helped the woman drink some more water. "The doctor will be back in five minutes. I'm sure he can do something for you."

The woman reached for Sadie's wrist and shook her head. "He can't help me. No one can."

"Don't talk like that. You're not dead yet. There's still hope."

"No. Not for me."

The door flung open and Sadie glanced over her shoulder, expecting to see the doctor but instead Jefferson came into the room, his face red, his hands clenched at his sides. His gray suit, which often made her think of storm clouds, matched his mood. And she knew why. Sadie inched closer to the sick woman, hoping he wouldn't hit her while they were in the presence of a lady.

"I had to take this lady to the doctor," Sadie quickly said. "She's very ill and needed help right away."

"She's here with the doctor," he growled and gestured to the door. "Madame requires your services at once."

"I can't leave her. Not like this."

"She's not your responsibility."

"But she has no family or friends. Someone needs to look after her."

He grabbed the back of her neck and squeezed it. Hard. "You will do as I say."

"St...stop," the woman croaked.

He immediately let go of Sadie who breathed a sigh of relief. "Don't be obstinate," he said through gritted teeth. "You won't like the consequences."

The doctor entered the room, his gaze going from Jefferson to Sadie then back to Jefferson. "Unless you're sick, you have no business being here," he told Jefferson.

He motioned to Sadie. "I'm here for Madame's property."

Sadie shot a pleading look to the doctor whose expression softened. "She's helping me with a patient. She'll go back to the brothel when she's done."

"That's not for you to decide," Jefferson snapped.

"It is as long as a patient's life hangs in the balance." The doctor set his medicine bag on his desk and gestured to the door. "The last thing my patient needs is needless bickering. Now go before I get the sheriff."

Straightening his shoulders, he stepped over to the doctor. "If you insist on keeping that whore here, then you'll need to pay Madame. We got a customer waiting for her and he's a big spender. She doesn't take the loss of income lightly."

The doctor glanced at Sadie for a moment then sighed. "Very well."

Sadie swallowed the lump in her throat. The doctor was a good man, an honorable one. And he'd seen firsthand how things were for the prostitutes at Madame's brothel. His kindness had been the only thing that didn't make Sadie give up after Jefferson had beaten her until she had the miscarriages.

As the doctor paid Jefferson, Sadie chanced a look at the woman, wondering if she'd witnessed the whole sordid conversation. To her dismay, the woman turned her tender gaze in her direction. Sadie quickly looked away and did what she could to muster what little dignity she had left, if there was any.

To her surprise, the woman touched her hand, causing her to make eye contact with her. The woman offered her a smile but then started coughing again.

Sadie hastened to help her sit up so she could get the blood out of her lungs. It was frightening to see how much blood could fill up a cloth in just a few coughs. Forgetting the discomfort from having Jefferson there, she gave the woman more water.

"I paid you, now go," the doctor told Jefferson.

"She's not worth the amount you paid but much obliged." Jefferson tipped his hat and left.

The doctor shook his head then turned to grab a bottle from a shelf. "I got something to help for that cough."

After he poured a spoonful of the medicine, he gave it to her and Sadie waited to see if it'd help. A few more coughs later, the woman settled down and relaxed.

"What is your name, Miss?" the doctor asked, his tender gaze on her.

"Hazel," she replied as Sadie helped her back on the bed and fluffed her pillow. "Hazel McPherson."

"Hazel, I'm afraid I have some bad news. Your condition is very serious, and—"

The door opened and an anxious young man came in. "There's been an accident. Right at the factory. We need your help."

The doctor glanced from the man to Hazel.

"Is he coming?" an older man asked, peering into the room.

"I know I'm not going to make it," Hazel softly said then swallowed. "Go on and save someone who has a chance."

"I'm sorry," he replied then grabbed his medical bag and followed the other men.

Outside, Sadie saw a flurry of activity. She was tempted to go over to the window to get a better look at the commotion but Hazel groaned and her attention went back to her. "Don't listen to him, Hazel. You might make it."

"No, I won't. I can feel my life slipping from me." Before Sadie could argue, she clasped her hand with surprising strength. "That man who came in here for you... Has he hurt you?"

Despite the warmth in Sadie's cheeks, she said, "What Jefferson's done is nothing compared to what you're going through. You don't need to mind any of that. The important thing is that you don't give up."

"The doctor's right. Nothing can save me. But," her eyes met Sadie's, "you can be saved." With a grimace, she gestured to the glass of water.

She hurried to give Hazel more to drink.

Releasing a shallow breath, she focused back on Sadie. "I don't have much time so please listen."

Sadie closed her mouth and leaned forward to hear her better.

"I'm supposed to be a mail-order bride, and I was on my way to marry Allen Grover. His letter is in my purse. He has a baby son who needs a mother. He's in Rapid City. The ticket and money needed for the trip is in the purse. I want you to go. Get a new start. Don't go back to the brothel. Go to Allen."

Sadie shook her head. "I can't do that."

"Do you want to be a prostitute for the rest of your life?"

She winced. "No. Of course not." What woman in her right mind would want to live that kind of life?

"Then go to Allen. He'll be good to you."

Sadie opened her mouth to protest but then she saw blood on Hazel's lips. Bolting to her feet, she grabbed a fresh cloth and dabbed it on her mouth. "Why are you so sick? Is it really pneumonia?" She wasn't a doctor, but something didn't seem right about any of this.

Hazel, unfortunately, never answered. She couldn't. Because the next breath was her last…

Sadie took a shaky breath and looked down at the dress she was sewing. By getting lost in her memories, she had messed up the seam she'd been working on. With a sigh, she set the dress down. She was due to meet Aunt Betty. And since Aunt Betty knew how to sew better than she did, she would implore upon the woman's kindness to teach her to do a better job.

She went over to Gilbert, who had settled on the floor with his blanket, and noticed he was asleep. With a chuckle, she picked him up, tucking the blanket around him, and took him to his crib. With a smile, she brushed back a lock of his blond hair. He was so much at peace. Al had been good to him, giving him a home where he felt safe enough to fall asleep anywhere.

She returned to the main living area and undid the sewing she'd done, careful to preserve the fabric. Al spent his hard-earned money on it, and the last thing she wanted to do was ruin it. After she returned the cloth and sewing supplies to the bedroom, Al came into the house with an excited expression on his face.

"Did you get something?" she asked, going over to him.

"I did. And it's a beauty, too. Aunt Betty can make a coat out of its hide for you once we get it cleaned up. She made a coat for me two years ago, and it's better than anything else I've owned. I usually barter for things from her."

"What do you barter?"

"I give her and her husband meat, milk, and wood in exchange for clothing and blankets. Tomorrow when we go over to her, I'll take the hide and some meat over."

"Alright." Since he hadn't brought anything in, she asked, "Where's the animal?"

"The elk is out on the table in the shed. You still want me to show you how I cut it up and preserve the meat?"

She nodded. The sooner she learned how to help do the chores around here, the better. "Gilbert's taking a nap so I have time to do it."

"Let me get you some things, and then we can get out there."

Curious, she followed him to the bedroom and watched as he retrieved one of his old shirts and gloves and handed them to her. "You'll want to protect that pretty dress of yours. I have an extra apron you can use out in the shed. You should also wear my boots. I know they won't fit well, but I don't want you wearing your nice ones." He slipped off his boots and handed them to her.

"What are you going to wear?"

"Another pair of socks."

"Won't that be uncomfortable?"

He shrugged and retrieved a second pair that he slipped on. "I'm used to the cold and the land. Don't worry. Once we start working, you'll barely notice how chilly it is out there."

She put on the shirt, boots and gloves then joined him as he went to the shed. The sunlight filtering through the trees gave them enough light through the window so they could see everything they needed to.

He slipped a heavy apron around her so that the part of her dress that wasn't covered by the shirt was protected. Then he gave her his hat. "For your hair," he explained when she shot him a questioning look.

"What about your hair?"

He shrugged. "I'll wash it up when we're done. You have longer hair than I do." He leaned forward and kissed her. "You're cute in my things."

"Am I?" She glanced down at what she was wearing and saw how big his clothes and boots looked on her.

"You are." He snapped his fingers and pulled a bandana out of his back pocket. "You might need this to block some of the smell."

"I could have used this for Gilbert's diaper change this morning."

He chuckled at her joke. "I didn't think of it, but yes, this would help for that, too. You might want to stand a little further back."

With a nod, she stepped where he indicated and spent the next hour watching as he skinned the elk and then cut up the meat. Several times, she had to step out of the shed to get some fresh air so she wouldn't vomit. She knew this was going to be disgusting, but she had underestimated just how much. But it was something she needed to know.

This was her new life. She was up for the challenge. No matter what she had to do or what she had to overcome, she would do it. It was much more preferable than her old life. Hazel had given her a second chance, and she was going to do everything she could to hold onto it, no matter what. And if that meant cutting up some meat and fighting back bouts of wanting to throw up, then so be it.

Chapter Eight

Al entered the bedroom that night and saw that Hazel was staring at the ceiling, the blanket pulled halfway up to her chest. She wore his shirt, but without her chemise, it was easy to see the outline of her breasts. Forcing his gaze to her face, he smiled.

"I promise it'll get easier to skin an animal," he told her. "Once you get over the blood and smell, there's nothing to it."

She directed her gaze to him and smiled. "Just like changing Gilbert's diaper?"

"Yes, though I will admit my pa taught me how to preserve animal meat and make things from the skin, so I grew up doing that."

He removed his clothes, except for the underwear, and slipped on his nightshirt. This time, he didn't ask her if she wanted the light on. He only dimmed it. He didn't know why she wanted the light on, but it was a small thing to oblige her. Maybe she was afraid of the dark. Or maybe it hinted at something about her past that she didn't want to talk about. Either way, he figured if keeping the light on made her feel safe, he was happy to do it.

He settled into the bed and smiled at her. "Are you happy here?"

"Yes." She hesitated then asked, "Are you happy with me being here?"

"Of course I am." He brought her into his arms and kissed her. Having taken care of himself just before dawn that morning, he could enter the bed and not be so hard it was uncomfortable. But even so, he felt the stirring of desire center in his loins and wished he'd taken the time to take care of himself before he came to bed tonight. Ending the kiss, he cleared his throat and focused on her beautiful face. "I just hope you never regret leaving Atlanta to be with me. I know cutting up an animal is a far cry from having servants at your beck and call."

"I don't regret coming here."

He studied her expression, trying to gauge what it was she wasn't telling him. He knew she was happy being here, but there was something under her words that hinted at something unpleasant. He brushed her cheek. "What was your life like in Atlanta?"

She shifted against him, probably not meaning to brush her thigh against his erection, but she did and it further aroused him. He shifted away from her, but she pulled him closer to her.

"We're in bed," she whispered, her breasts pressing against his chest and her hips intimately pressed against his. "Why don't you consummate the marriage? We can talk later."

Before he could respond, she kissed him. The kiss felt as wonderful as everything else about her, and he found himself giving into the urge to deepen it. She cupped the side of his face and traced his lower lip with her tongue, slipping into his mouth when he parted his lips for her. How he wanted to give in and fully enjoy her, to learn what it was like to make love to a woman, to experience the ecstasy of releasing his seed inside her instead of always doing it on the ground. He'd only imagined what it'd be like, but it had to be one of the most pleasurable experiences anyone could have.

He traced the curves of her body, recalling how she'd looked when he'd explored her on their wedding night. He wanted to see her again, of course. He didn't think he'd ever get tired of feasting his eyes on her bare flesh, but at the moment he was too caught up in feeling her. With his eyes closed, he was more aware of the softness of her breasts and the curve of her hip. His hand went lower and he touched the edge of the shirt. Slipping his hand under it, he realized she wasn't wearing anything under it and let out a groan. She parted her legs and he brought his hand to her most secret place. When he found her entrance, he slid a finger into it. Her flesh pulled him in deeper.

Maybe he should consummate their marriage tonight. She was holding him and encouraging him to continue by interlacing her tongue with his. Everything seemed to be right. She was willing to receive him, and it would be a simple thing to pull down his underwear and enter her. Chances were, he wouldn't last long. He already felt close to release. It would be quick and then her worries about what to expect from this would be resolved. She'd undoubtedly feel better about facing the uncertainty in the whole thing, and he didn't want her to keep going through the question of what to expect every time they came to bed.

But something wasn't right. Yes, he figured she'd be a little tense since she was nervous, but there seemed to be something deeper than that. And no matter how hard he tried, he couldn't pin it down.

"I'm sorry," he whispered as he slid his finger out of her and shifted so that they weren't so close. "I just can't do it."

"Sure you can. You're hard." Her hand went to his erection and he groaned. That felt much better than when he touched himself. She ran her hand down his shaft. "You're fully capable of doing it."

As much as it pained him, he removed her hand. "The timing isn't right," he forced out despite his raspy breathing.

"Sure it is."

She rolled on top of him and pushed his underwear down. "I'm ready for you. I can take you in."

He stopped her before she could take him inside her. "No." He quickly rolled back onto his side, careful that she landed softly on the bed. "It doesn't feel right. It feels like you're forcing this."

"That's ridiculous. A woman can't force these things."

Noting the blush in her cheeks, he paused and tried to think of the best way to explain it. "You're not ready. Emotionally. You need more time."

"I need more time? All I need is to be wet enough for you to get the job done, and I'm wet. I don't understand you. Why did you ask for a mail-order bride if you didn't plan to do this? Why not ask for a nanny for your son instead?"

He winced. "I don't think of you as a nanny."

"No? That's all I've been since I came here. All I do is take care of Gilbert and tidy up around the house."

"You're more than that. You're my wife."

"Then why don't you treat me like one?"

"I will when the time is right."

"And when will that be?"

"I don't know."

"You don't know? I don't understand you at all. What's there to know? We said the vows. There's nothing else to do."

He tried to explain what he was waiting for, but he didn't completely understand it himself. "I'm sorry. I wish I could explain it, but I can't."

She stared at him for a long moment then let out a huff and turned onto her side, her back to him.

The tension was thick in the room, and for the life of him, he couldn't grasp what he'd said or done to upset her so much. And he sensed now wasn't the time to ask. He'd be better off waiting until tomorrow when everything calmed down. After a moment, he dared to ask, "Do you want me to sleep somewhere else tonight?"

"That depends on whether or not it's the right time to do it," she muttered.

He already knew she wouldn't let him hold her. Not tonight anyway. Turning his back to her, he stared at the wall, wondering what he did to upset her and how he could make it better.

He didn't fall asleep for a long time. He wasn't sure if she did either. He heard her steady breathing. So maybe she had. Several times, he wanted to roll over and hold her, if nothing else than to be reassured that she'd forgive him. But he didn't think she'd welcome his touch at the moment so he didn't. Finally, he was able to drift off into a fitful sleep.

***

Sadie woke up before Al did the next morning, and she quietly left the bedroom. She carried the kerosene lamp out with her since it was still dark out. He didn't mind the dark, but she did. She always wanted to know what was going on around her. Too many bad things could be hiding in the shadows.

She put some wood in the cookstove to warm up the room then cleaned up around the place, trying to do everything she could to avoid thinking about last night and the argument she'd had with Al. She didn't want to argue with him. The days had been so pleasant since she came here. But it seemed as if she couldn't help messing things up.

Why couldn't he just finish consummating the marriage? Then she wouldn't have to keep living in dread of when he'd finally get around to it. It was worse because she couldn't tell him why she wanted him to get it over with. Of all the times she'd spent wishing men wouldn't need to give into their baser urges, it had to be with the only one who was actually allowed to.

As she dusted the shelves, she reminded herself that Al didn't know how much she dreaded it. He thought she was a virgin and, therefore, uncertain of what to expect. She wished she was a virgin. Being uncertain would be much easier to cope with. How she wished she didn't know the way men used women for their selfish pleasure.

Setting the cloth down, she went over to sit in the rocking chair and placed her face in her hands. This wasn't the person she wanted to be. She was becoming bitter and she didn't like it. She'd fought that part of herself from time to time. It was easy to give in and let bitterness take over. Then she'd be as cold and unloving as her mother had been when she'd been consumed by bitterness after her father's death. So consumed, in fact, that she'd dropped Sadie off and never looked back, despite Sadie's cries for her to come back. Or as bitter as Jefferson who used people to get whatever he wanted. She saw the fruits that came from a life of bitterness.

She shivered. That wasn't the kind of person she wanted to be. She wanted to be a blessing to Al and Gilbert. She wanted them to be glad whenever they saw her. She wanted Gilbert to raise his hands in hopes she'd hold him when she entered the room. She wanted to be worthy of their love.

Releasing her breath, she straightened in the chair and studied the small cabin. It was still quiet since Al and Gilbert were sleeping. This place, for all its simplicity, was one of peace. She could be happy here. She had been happier here than she'd been since her pa died. This could be a place of joy and laughter if she'd only open herself to it.

And that meant she'd have to wait for Al to be ready to consummate the marriage. She couldn't force it. She'd just have to go through each day and live with the dread. It wasn't a sacrifice. Not when she had endured having a man take his pleasure with her many nights in the past. She could do this. She just needed to stop dwelling on it.

The bedroom door creaked open and she turned her gaze in time to see Al peek out. Despite the tense argument they'd had, she caught a chuckle rising up in her throat. "You can come out here," she whispered so Gilbert wouldn't wake up.

He opened the door further and stepped into the light. Too late, she realized she was only wearing one of his shirts, and that hardly covered her legs. She cleared her throat and tucked the shirt around her thighs as much as possible. For some reason, she didn't feel it was appropriate to be in such a state of undress around him. Of all the men she might feel a shred of modesty with, she didn't think it'd be her own husband.

He walked over to her and knelt in front of her. Taking her hands in his, his gaze met hers. "I'm sorry."

It took her a moment to realize he was actually apologizing to her. "Al, you have nothing to be sorry for."

"I keep turning you down. It's not fair of me to make the judgment of whether or not the time is right for us to be intimate. If you want to do it, we should."

"Really?"

"It's both of us in this marriage. Your say needs to have equal pull with mine."

Her initial reaction was relief. She could get it over with and stop worrying about it. But then would she be any better than the men who'd forced their will upon her in the past? It hadn't mattered to them if she wanted to do it. They wanted it and that was all they cared about.

She opened her mouth to answer him when Gilbert's cry came from the other room.

"Let me take care of him this morning," Al said then rose to his feet. "You should go back to bed and get some more rest."

"I'm not tired. And besides," she glanced at the window "the sun's coming up."

"Alright, but if you need to rest today, I hope you do especially since we're supposed to go to Aunt Betty's for supper." He headed for Gilbert's room then stopped. "Of course, we don't have to. I can always go over there and tell her we're not coming if you're too tired."

She thought about taking him up on his offer since she wasn't looking forward to meeting a woman who could tell whether or not someone was a good person just by meeting them. But Al was being so gracious to her, giving her freedoms that she never dreamt a man would give a woman. The least she could do was meet his friend. "I want to go," she finally said.

He smiled. "She'll like you."

As he turned to go to Gilbert's room, she could only hope he was right.

Chapter Nine

Sadie would be lying if she didn't admit that she was a bundle of nerves. It wasn't that she considered herself shy around new people. Certainly, she'd been around enough of them, men and women. But from what she gathered about Aunt Betty, she was a decent woman—one who'd always done everything right. Could such a woman figure out Sadie wasn't the person she was pretending to be?

Releasing her breath, she finished brushing her hair then pulled it back into a bun. After pinning the bun in place, she gathered her hat and slipped it over her head. She took a step back and inspected her reflection in the mirror. She looked very much like a lady, someone proper and decent, someone who would be a good match for a gentleman like Al. But when she lifted her gaze to her face, the reality of who she was struck her hard. Whore. That was exactly the type of lady she'd been. This dress, the taking of Hazel's name, this matter of being a wife... It didn't change anything about her past. About who she truly was.

"I don't belong here," she whispered then sat on the bed before her knees gave out.

She quickly brushed her tears away, silently demanding they stop. She hated crying. It seemed that most of her life, that's all she'd done. And she was tired of it. All she wanted was to be happy.

"What's so wrong with that?" she asked aloud.

But no one could answer the question, least of all her.

A gentle tapping at the bedroom door brought her attention to Al who poked his head into the room. "The horse and wagon are out front. You ready?"

Forcing a smile, she nodded and rose to her feet. Despite the slight shaking in her legs, she managed to cross the room so she stood before him. She cleared her throat and took a deep breath. "I'm ready."

To her surprise, he slipped his arm around her shoulders and pulled her close to his side. "You have nothing to worry about. Aunt Betty will like you."

"You can tell I'm nervous?"

"Don't be embarrassed. It's natural to be nervous." He gave her shoulders a light squeeze then kissed her cheek. "I'll get Gilbert then we'll go to the wagon, alright?"

He released her and she slowly headed for the door. She shouldn't be surprised he detected her mood, but she thought she did a better job of masking her feelings than that.

She took her shawl from the hook and slipped it around her shoulders. She really needed to get a handle on her emotions. If she wasn't careful, Al would suspect she wasn't Hazel. She was already pressing her luck by not consummating their marriage. Not that she hadn't tried. But for some reason, he kept insisting they needed to wait until the time was right. She didn't understand that at all. Since when did men need the time to be right to be intimate with a woman?

The door behind her shut, and she turned to see Al holding a bundled up Gilbert. This time when she smiled, she didn't have to force it. The two looked so cute together, and Al was such a good father. It was refreshing to see a man who cared about someone other than himself.

"I'll take him," she said, holding her arms out to the little boy.

He handed Gilbert to her and they headed for the wagon. After he helped her in, she settled the boy on her lap and tucked the hood closer around his face. When he looked up at her, he shot her such a heartwarming smile that more tears sprang up in her eyes. But these were tears of joy and they felt so wonderful compared to the other kind. Truly, she wouldn't mind this kind of crying.

"He likes you," Al said.

Her gaze shifted to Al. "Pardon?"

"Gilbert's taken a liking to you."

"Oh, he's just a baby. He's trusting of everyone."

"Well, there's no denying he already thinks of you as his ma."

"I am his ma." And that felt good to say. She tucked a few errant strands of his blond curls back into the hood then wrapped him in a protective hug. "I had no idea it could feel so good to be a mother."

Al winked at her before he released the brake and led the horse forward. "You're a natural at it."

Pleased, she turned her attention back to the boy and studied his expression as he took in the trees around them. For him, everything in the world was new and fresh. The future loomed in front of him, ripe with adventure and excitement. It was easy to forget the past when she saw the world through his eyes.

Al took them down the path, and instead of taking them down the way that led to town, he went in the opposite direction. "Do you go to Aunt Betty's often?" she asked, wondering how many times Gilbert had been this way.

"More often than not, she comes over to my home, especially after I found Gilbert."

Her eyebrows furrowed. "Found Gilbert?"

"You remember what I told you about him in the letter I wrote you?"

She wanted to say no because she didn't read any of the letters he sent Hazel, but she knew she couldn't. Not without giving herself away. How did he end up with Gilbert?

"Um...of course," she finally replied. If Hazel hadn't been so ill, Sadie was sure she would have told her what she knew about Al.

They came upon another twist in the path, and he took a left. "We're almost there."

Gilbert squirmed in her arms so she set him up, allowing him to get a better view of their surroundings.

"I'm glad you can hold him while we go on these trips," Al said, motioning to the boy who babbled in contentment. "He was getting bored having to lie down in his bassinet all the time."

"He's curious about the world. Everything is brand new to him," she commented. "Everything must be exciting for him."

"It probably is."

Up ahead a cabin larger than the one Al owned came into view. "I'm guessing that's Aunt Betty's house?"

"It is. There are a few houses around the area, but they're easy to miss when you consider all the trees."

Gilbert continued his happy babbling as they came up to the house with two stories to it and a large porch. Out front, a dog barked a greeting but stayed by the two girls who were playing. One was pushing the other on a swing that hung from a sturdy tree limb. An older boy, who was whittling something from where he sat on the porch, glanced up then hurried into the house.

"Aunt Betty's got four children still living with her. The others are already on their own," Al explained.

"How many children does she have?"

"Ten."

Her jaw dropped. "Ten?"

"She jokes that all her husband has to do is look at her and she's expecting again."

"Usually, I'd say that is silly, but considering she has ten, I think he should stop looking at her."

He chuckled and pulled the horses to a stop. "Seeing as how he's always talking about how pretty she is, I don't think that's going to happen any time soon."

She waited for him to come around to her side of the wagon and let him help her down.

"Is this your bride?" a young girl called out as she ran up to them.

"Yep," Al replied. "She's the best thing that's ever happened to me."

Sadie detected the pride in his voice and looked at him, a flicker of guilt threatening to emerge from the place she had successfully pushed it down. He was really paying the high compliment to the woman he assumed Sadie was, not to the person she really was. Hazel would deserve the praise, no doubt. She didn't think he'd sound so happy if he knew the truth about her.

Pushing aside the unease, she returned his smile then looked at the girl. "Al is a wonderful husband. No woman could ask for a better one."

He placed his hand on the small of her back and kissed her cheek. "Thank you."

The front door of the cabin creaked open and a plump woman waved to them. "Don't be a stranger, you two. Come on in and make yourself at home."

"Guess who that is," Al said, turning his gaze back to Sadie.

Though there was no one else it could be, given the woman's cheerful demeanor, Sadie decided to answer him. "Aunt Betty."

"She can't wait to meet you," the girl chirped.

"I'll bring in your cloth and sewing kit. You go on in," Al told her.

Taking a deep breath, she nodded and followed the girl to the cabin. She walked with her up the steps and glanced back in time to see Al picking up a crate from the back of the wagon. Then her gaze went to the boy and other girl who watched her. Did they figure out she wasn't really Hazel? Did children have a sixth sense about these things?

"What a pleasure it is to meet you!"

Sadie's attention went to Aunt Betty who embraced her. "Al told us all about you. Well," she chuckled and patted Sadie's arm, "only what you told him in the letters of course. I hope you don't mind. He was so excited when he finally got a reply, he came right over to tell me that he found the woman he'd be spending the rest of his life with."

"I don't mind," Sadie assured her as she followed her into the cabin. The aroma of biscuits, a cherry pie, and a roast made her mouth water. "It smells good in here."

"Ma's known for her good cooking," an older girl—probably sixteen—said as she hurried to set the dining table.

"I love it. It's my passion in life," Aunt Betty said, her smile growing wider. "Besides taking care of my family, of course." Her gaze went to Gilbert and she rubbed his back. "You're getting bigger all the time. Before you know it," her gaze went back to Sadie, "he'll be walking all over the place."

Would he? Sadie had no idea when babies started walking.

"He's already taken a liking to you," Aunt Betty continued. "I told Al that if Gilbert took a liking to the woman who came up here to marry him, then he'd better get her to a preacher right away. Babies don't lie. They know who the good ones are."

Did that mean Sadie met her approval? But how could the woman know anything about her, other than what was in the letters? And just how much had Hazel written? Too bad she hadn't been able to read Hazel's letters when she found them in the house.

"Al told me you aren't familiar with sewing," Aunt Betty said, drawing Sadie's attention back to her.

"I can do simple patterns," Sadie replied. "But I can't make a shirtwaist or a skirt."

"Would you like to learn?"

"You wouldn't mind teaching me?"

"Mind?" her daughter called out as she set a plate on the table. "She'd be in heaven."

"Missy is right," Aunt Betty agreed. "I love to sew, too."

Sadie couldn't help but be in awe of this woman who had so much enthusasm. Was there anything she didn't love doing?

Gilbert yawned and the woman chuckled. "Would you mind if he takes a nap in the other room? I still have a crib for when my older children bring the grandchildren over."

With a nod, Sadie handed Gilbert to her.

As Aunt Betty carried the boy to another room, Missy set down the last plate and walked over to her. "Was it scary to leave Atlanta?"

"Oh, well…" Did Hazel look scared when she found her sitting alone in the restaurant? Sadie didn't think so. She had seemed worried, perhaps. But not scared. "I wasn't scared," she slowly ventured, "but I did wonder what kind of man I had agreed to marry." And that was true. Sadie did wonder what Al was like the whole time she was on her way up here.

"You chose a good one. He's wonderful."

Sadie caught the wistful tone in the girl's voice. Missy was in love with him. "How old are you?"

"I'll be sixteen next month."

Feeling a little better, Sadie relaxed. She was still a child. She had no doubt Al saw her that way. And she had no doubt that Missy would outgrow her schoolgirl infatuation and fall in love with someone else. But Sadie could see why the girl felt the way she did. Al was a good man—a decent man. It'd be hard not to love him.

"You sure go through a lot of trouble for us," a man said as he stepped into the cabin.

Sadie turned and saw a large man close to Aunt Betty's age carrying a crate into the cabin. Al followed close behind, carrying another crate. Thankful for the change in topic while the men set the crates on the floor by a chair, Sadie looked at Missy. "Is that your pa?"

"Yes. He's a bear of a man, isn't he?" Missy leaned closer to her and giggled. "We nicknamed him 'Bear' for that reason."

Sadie thought the nickname suited him just right. He was as big as one, and he had thick, dark hair and a beard that were starting to gray. When he hurried over to say hello and shake her hand, he had a nice, strong grip.

"It's a pleasure to meet you, Hazel," he said, just as friendly as Aunt Betty had been. "Name's Nel, but people call me Bear."

Forcing a smile at being called Hazel, she returned the greeting. "Nice to meet you, Bear."

"I got your cloth and sewing kit on the chair in that room," Al told Sadie, patting the small of her back.

"Thank you," she replied.

"Want to check the traps with me?" Bear asked Al.

Al nodded but tipped his hat to greet Missy before he headed back outside with Bear.

Sadie sensed that Al knew Missy had a fondness for him, but to his credit, he didn't do anything to encourage it. He managed to be polite without making her think anything would ever come of her feelings. A man Al's age could easily impress a girl so young, and Sadie had been around enough men to know some would be more than happy to take advantage of a young girl's feelings. But not Al. Al would never use anyone.

Aunt Betty came out of the other room. "I see the men brought in your sewing supplies. How much time do we have before supper?" she asked Missy.

"A half hour," Missy replied.

"Hmm... It's not a lot of time, but it's enough to get started." Aunt Betty gestured to one of the chairs. "The men will want to sit on the porch and talk for a while after we eat. We'll get a lot more done then. But there's no reason why we can't get started now."

"I am eager to learn how to make more than a simple dress," Sadie admitted.

"You came to the right house."

Relaxing, Sadie settled into one of the chairs and pulled out the blue cloth she'd been eager to work on. It was silly how she worried about coming here. Aunt Betty and her family were nicer than she'd ever dreamed. No wonder Al spoke so highly of them. And the fact that they spoke so highly of him spoke volumes about his character. Yes, she was truly fortunate that she got to marry him. Hazel had picked the best man possible, and she'd always be grateful to Hazel for it.

***

That night after Sadie tucked Gilbert into bed, she went to her bedroom and saw that Al was removing his pants. He glanced at her. "Would you like me to come to bed without anything on?"

She knew what he was asking. He wanted to know if she wanted him to consummate their marriage. She closed the distance between them and rose on her toes so she could kiss his cheek. "You're such a wonderful man," she whispered.

"Is that a yes or a no?" he asked with a chuckle.

"Al, I'm sorry about last night. You're right. The timing isn't right and when we finally do it, I want it to be right for both of us." Because that's what he deserved. He deserved the best. He asked so little of others but gave so much, and people like him were too often taken for granted. "I've never met anyone like you. You're the most wonderful man who's ever lived."

His face grew pink. "Why do I get the feeling that Aunt Betty made me out to be better than I am?"

"She did no such thing. I gathered that all on my own. You're a good man. I didn't know men like you existed until I got here. I'm glad I'm your wife."

He cupped her face in his hands and smiled. "I'm glad I'm your husband."

"Will you hold me while we sleep?"

He nodded. "I enjoy holding you."

She still didn't understand how a man could hold a woman through the night without fulfilling the desires of the flesh, but he'd proven he could do it. With a smile, she gave him a chaste kiss before she got ready for bed.

Chapter Ten

Two weeks passed and Sadie finally finished the shirtwaist and skirt. Excited, she put the outfit on after she bathed and inspected her reflection in the mirror. The high neckline trimmed in lace and accented with a cameo Al had bought for her only enhanced the image standing before her. She pinned her hair back into an attractive style and stood back once more, making sure it was all real—that she wasn't dreaming.

A smile crossed her face and she turned to make sure she looked as good from the back. And she did. She felt just like a princess in a fairytale. For the first time in her life, she believed she was a lady. An honest to goodness lady. So this was what it felt like to be a wife. No wonder the wives she used to pass in Nebraska were always smiling. Being a wife was an incredibly liberating experience. Dignified, virtuous, pure. Being Al's wife had made this possible.

A flicker of guilt crossed her reflection, and she couldn't bear to look at herself anymore. She was an imposter. She wasn't really a lady. It was all a ruse. She was a prostitute. With a glance at her new clothes, she was tempted to rip it all to shreds. Gripping the edge of her skirt in her hands, she was ready to tear it along the seam when she heard the bedroom door open.

Jerking her head up, she turned and faced Al whose smile grew wide at the sight of her. "You're absolutely stunning," he said, motioning to her. "The men in Atlanta must have been falling all over themselves to get your attention." Before she could answer, he closed the distance between them and kissed her hands. "I'm the luckiest man in the world."

No, no he wasn't. Perhaps if he'd been with Hazel, he would have been. But not with her. Clearing her throat, she released her hands from his and forced a smile. "You're much too kind."

As she turned back to the mirror, she made a pretense of lining up the comb, barrettes, and ribbons on the dresser.

Wrapping his arms around her waist, he kissed her neck, an action which startled her. She returned her gaze to the mirror and was struck by how tender he was. But that was his way. Tender. Sweet. Always giving. Never expecting anything in return.

"Why are you so nice to me?" she whispered.

Glancing up at her reflection, he chuckled. "Pardon?"

"You have yet to insist on your right to consummate the marriage, and yet, you treat me as if I'm the most wonderful woman in the world."

Settling his chin on her shoulder, he gave her waist a light squeeze. "We didn't get a chance to know each other before we got married. I want to make sure when we do come together, the time will be right."

Lowering her gaze, she let out a soft laugh. "I would have thought performing our vows would have been the right time."

"Our vows did bring us together as husband and wife. But only time can bring our hearts into the same union."

Quickly blinking her tears away, she turned around to face him. "You have a noble heart, Al. You should have been a knight."

"No, I wouldn't have wanted that." He kissed the top of her nose. "If I had been born in that time, I wouldn't have met you." He patted the small of her back. "I better check on the eggs. I don't want them to burn."

He kissed her cheek then left the room.

She brushed away a tear as it trickled down her cheek. If he knew who she really was, he wouldn't be so eager to compliment her.

***

A week later, Sadie wiped the sweat from her forehead as she washed the dishes after supper. Had Gilbert not been awake and playing on the rocking chair, she would have opened the window to cool things off. But she wanted to keep the heat in the house from the cookstove going for his sake. She paused and looked over at the boy who was taking delight in rocking himself back and forth. His blanket, which was on the floor by the chair, had been forgotten but Sadie had no doubt he'd remember it before bed.

She smiled and resumed washing her dishes. The boy was such a sweet child. She didn't know if all children were sweet like him, but she couldn't recall a time when she felt so complete. She was his mother. After she was done with the dishes, she put them on the towel to dry and decided to see if Al needed more hot water for his bath.

Making sure Gilbert was still playing in the chair, she crossed the room and got ready to knock on the door when she heard a soft moan come from the room. She stopped and waited. She knew what the sound meant. She'd heard that sound many times over the past few years. It was the sound of a man receiving pleasure, though not at the point of climax…yet.

She softly opened the door to see what he was doing. He couldn't be with another woman. Her gaze went to the bathtub where he was stroking his erection. He let out another moan as his seed spilled over his hand and into the water. Her eyebrows furrowed. How long had he been doing this? And why would he take care of his needs when she'd made the offer—several times—to take care of them for him?

What a ridiculous question. She knew why. He sensed she didn't want to be intimate with him. And he was right. Despite her efforts to get him to be with her that way, she didn't really want to do it. How he picked that up, she didn't know. Maybe it was because he actually cared about her. Not all the men who stepped through a brothel were bad. But all of them knew she didn't care about them and none cared about her. It was understood that she'd provide a service and they would go on their way after that.

But with Al, it wasn't the same. He intended to be with her forever. That being the case, it was probably important to him that she truly wanted to be with him when they finally did it. Maybe she should have been upset, but it touched her that he'd rather take care of his own needs than do something that made her uncomfortable. Al was such a special person. She couldn't think of any other man who'd give up something he wanted for her sake.

With a quick glance at Gilbert to make sure he was still on the chair, she softly shut the door. She waited for a minute then knocked on the door. "Al?"

"Come in," he called out.

She opened the door and saw that he was already out of the tub, drying off with a towel. "I was going to ask if you wanted more hot water, but I can see you're done with your bath."

"Yeah, I just got out." He wrapped the towel around his waist and headed over to the dresser. "It was nice of you to think of me."

Making sure Gilbert was content, she closed the door behind her and approached him. "You deserve good things."

He smiled at her as he combed his hair. "I have good things. I have a roof over my head, food on the table, clothes on my back. And better yet, I have a wonderful wife and a happy son. I can't think of much else a man could want."

"Money, power, more land?"

He shrugged. "I don't know. It seems to me that the more you have, the more complicated things can get. But I take it that's what was important to the men you were used to in Atlanta?"

"Power was the biggest thing," she offered, though it was the power of a woman's fate that seemed to mean the most to a particular few, especially Jefferson.

"Well, I think power is an illusion. You can't really control anyone or anything except for yourself."

"I suppose."

He placed the comb on the dresser and turned to her. "You disagree?"

She shrugged. "I understand what you're saying. People can't control whether a person likes them or not, but they can control whether or not a person does something. If a person is sold into something, what choice does that person have?"

"You mean like a slave?"

Or a prostitute whose mother sold her into the business. What could a child possibly do in a situation like that? What could the child control out of any of it? But instead of asking those questions, she settled for nodding. "Yes, like a slave. Someone who was sold to a master and had no choice but to serve him. Because if he didn't, his master hunted him down and did something like cut off his foot so he wouldn't run away again. What about him?"

"I guess there are some things people can physically control, but one thing no one can control, no matter how hard they try, is the heart."

And he wanted her heart. Blinking back her tears, she cupped the side of his face with her hands and brought his mouth to hers so she could kiss him. It was the first time she ever kissed a man because she really wanted to.

He didn't respond at first, most likely because she shocked him. But then he warmed up to her and brought her into his arms to deepen the kiss. For the first time, she enjoyed it. Enjoyed the way his soft lips pressed against hers, the tentative brush of his tongue along her lower lip, and the gentle way his tongue interlaced with hers. She didn't think she would ever like a kiss. She didn't mind the kisses Al had given her up to this point, but this time was different. This time an unfamiliar thrill shot straight through her.

When she ended the kiss, it was with surprising reluctance. How she wanted to continue kissing him, but she heard Gilbert babbling and knew she had to tend to him. Her gaze met Al's and she smiled. "I better get him ready for bed." This time she kissed his cheek.

He returned her smile. "I'm looking forward to holding you tonight."

"I'm looking forward to it, too." And for the first time, she realized the bed could be a very nice place to spend time in.

***

Another week passed and the first snowfall of the season came. Sadie welcomed it. Being tucked away in a cozy cabin with Al and Gilbert was like being hidden from the rest of the world. At times, she liked to pretend it was just them and that she had come into the marriage without a tainted past. She liked to think her life didn't truly start until she had stepped off that stagecoach.

One morning while Al went out to take care of the animals, she decided to help Gilbert stand up. The boy might only be seven months old, but he was already showing how determined he was to explore more of the world around him. Part of that determination led to him trying to pull himself up on everything around him. So she would often oblige him by putting her hands around his and helping him to his feet. This earned her a big smile which made her chuckle.

"You're doing good," she told him when he was standing on his feet.

He leaned forward and she held onto his hands to help him maintain his balance. His legs gave out and she picked him up.

"You'll get there," she assured him as she rubbed his back. "Before you know it, you'll be running all over the place."

He reached out and touched her face. His fingers tickled her cheek and she chuckled again.

"I wish you could always be innocent," she whispered. "Don't be in a hurry to grow up."

There was a knock at the door, followed by a cheerful, "It's Aunt Betty."

"I'm coming," Sadie called out and carried the boy over with her. She opened the door and blinked in surprise when she saw the folded up clothes and a quilt in Aunt Betty's arms. "I hope you didn't go through a lot of trouble for us."

Aunt Betty glanced at the items in her arms and waved her concerns aside. "It was no trouble at all. My daughters help me make these, and between the three of us, we're quick. Besides, Al does such a good job of giving us good meat and sharing his vegetables and fruits. In return, I've been making clothes and blankets for him." She glanced at the window and sighed. "I should add curtains to the list. What color do you like most?"

"Blue. It reminds me of the sky." Never mind why. Aunt Betty didn't need to know the reason. To Sadie, it now represented freedom. Freedom from Nebraska. Freedom from prostitution. Freedom to be a wife. And not just anyone's wife. She was Al's wife. And she couldn't think of anything better than that. Returning her attention to Aunt Betty, she smiled. "Blue makes me think of Al."

Aunt Betty let out a squeal of delight and clasped her arm. "This is so exciting! That boy is head over heels in love with you."

She wanted to ask the woman what made her say that, but the woman went over to the worktable and lifted up a pink shirtwaist.

"I'm partial to cheerful colors, myself," Aunt Betty said. "This color will look lovely with your face. You have a natural pink hue in your cheeks." Giggling, she set it on the table. "You're such a beautiful woman. It's no wonder Al was smitten with you as soon as he saw you."

Sadie returned her smile. Other people—most notably Madame and Jefferson—had commented on her beauty in the past, but they saw it as something to use for their advantage. Madame insisted men pay more for the privilege of being with her, saying that having a prettier girl should be worth more. Madame was not so nice to look upon, but she prided herself on her keen business sense. And besides, she never slept with any of the men who walked through the doors. No. She'd never degrade herself that way, Sadie thought with a twinge of bitterness.

"This is for Gilbert."

Surprised her mind had drifted to places she didn't want it to be, Sadie turned her attention back to Aunt Betty and saw the small shirt and pants. "They're wonderful." She stroked Gilbert's back. "What do you think, Gilbert? You like it?"

He reached for it, so Sadie obliged him and stepped closer to the clothes so he could touch them. But he gripped them and tried to pull them into his mouth.

Aunt Betty giggled and gently removed his hand from the clothes. "He's a baby. They love to put everything in their mouths." She patted his head. "And this little one is so precious. A real gift, I tell you."

"Yes, he is."

"Poor Al. He was at a loss when he found him. He didn't know anything about caring for babies. A man can hardly prepare for it when he stumbles upon a baby who's been left in the woods all alone."

"Al found Gilbert in the woods?" Sadie asked in surprise.

Aunt Betty stopped going through the pile and turned to her. "Didn't he tell you?"

"Well, um… He told me a little bit but not much," Sadie ventured, hoping she wouldn't arouse Aunt Betty's suspicions.

"The poor man was beside himself when he came to my door with Gilbert. Gilbert had just been born and was wrapped in a blanket by a tree. Al was out hunting at the time and heard a baby crying. There was no note or anything telling any of us who the baby was or who he belonged to."

"You mean, the mother just left the baby out there to die?"

"Or the father. It's impossible to know who left the baby out there."

"That's awful," she whispered.

"Al felt sorry for the little one. I was willing to take Gilbert in and raise him as one of my own, but Al felt like he was meant to do it since he was the one who found him." She chuckled. "Al's a romantic. He believes in destiny and fate and all that. You married a good one. If I'd been single and younger, I would have married him myself." She winked at her. "But I wouldn't trade my Bear for anyone."

Sadie smiled at the woman before turning her gaze back to Gilbert who rested in her arms. This poor little boy had been abandoned and left for dead. Swallowing the lump in her throat, she kissed the top of his head and rubbed his back. Whoever had given birth to him didn't matter. What mattered was that he was going to have a good future.

"Thank you for coming all the way up here to marry Al," Aunt Betty said. "As soon as he found Gilbert, he went right out and posted the ad, but no one responded until you did. I think a lot of ladies would rather be in a bigger town than so far out this way, and who can blame them? It's a sacrifice to give up the nice things they're used to. But it's sure nice you didn't let that deter you."

"It was no sacrifice to come here, Aunt Betty," Sadie whispered, glancing at Gilbert. "It was the best thing that ever happened to me."

Aunt Betty smiled and turned back to the other items on the worktable. "You're a very special person."

"Thank you," Sadie forced out, wishing that was really true.

"Now," the woman began as she lifted a shirt, "this is for Al. Oh, he did mention how you need a better pair of boots for living out here, so I got one of my boys on that. And you don't need to worry. He makes the best boots around so you can trust him to do a good job."

As Aunt Betty continued talking, Sadie continued to stroke Gilbert's back, thinking that she was very fortunate to be able to step in the role as his mother. She'd never take him or Al or anything in this new life for granted.

Chapter Eleven

That evening, Sadie held Gilbert in the rocking chair, staring at the sweetest smile she'd even seen. They were both so much alike…both of them having gone through abandonment by those who were supposed to love them. Tears filled her eyes as she caressed his cheek.

He looked up at her, and she wiped more tears as they fell down her face. Then he laughed in a way that indicated he wanted her to be happy, to laugh along with him.

She leaned forward and kissed his forehead. "I'll tell you what. I'll do the crying for both of us and you can do the laughing."

Swallowing the lump in her throat, she hurried over to the kitchen so she could get his bottle ready. When she returned, she picked him up in her arms and settled back into the chair. He was content to drink his last meal of the day while she slowly rocked him back and forth.

She brushed a part of his hair from his forehead, pleased to watch him as he continued to drink his meal.

The front door opened and Al came into the cabin. "Is he asleep?" he whispered.

"Almost," she replied then returned her gaze to Gilbert whose eyes were closed. "It won't be long."

He put his hat on the hook then shut the door. As she watched him take off his coat, she couldn't help but think he had the biggest heart of anyone she'd ever met. She couldn't think of any other man who'd take in a baby to raise as his own.

Clearing her throat, she nodded toward the worktable. "I made you some tea. It's supposed to relax you at bedtime."

"You didn't have to do that," he replied as he took off his boots.

"I know but I wanted to. Besides, all I had to do was boil some water and add the herbs. It wasn't like I performed some great feat."

He chuckled at her joke and went to retrieve the cup. "Well, I appreciate it. The air's getting chillier. Winter's not too far off."

"No, it's not." And she liked that. She was looking forward to the land being covered in snow, especially when a fresh layer of it covered the tree branches.

"Did you celebrate Christmas in Atlanta?"

Lowering her gaze, she focused on Gilbert as he finished the bottle. "Who doesn't?"

Even Madame celebrated it. She said it was the ideal time to take care of lonely men. And it was one of the busiest nights of the year. Sadie used to hate it. But in this cabin with Al and Gilbert, it just might be something she could look forward to.

"I already got you a gift," Al said, a teasing tone in his voice.

She made eye contact with him and smiled. "You going to give me a hint?"

"Nope." With a satisfied grin, he finished the tea and set the cup down.

"That's not very nice of you. If you're going to say you got me something, the least you can do is give me an idea of what it is."

"If I did that, it wouldn't be a surprise. And what's the fun of a present if you can't be surprised?"

"But if you give me a good hint, then I won't figure out what it is."

He shook his head. "Sorry. You won't get me to talk. Trust me, you'll be glad you waited when Christmas day comes."

Amused, she turned her attention back to Gilbert as Al went to the bedroom to get ready for bed. Gilbert had been fighting sleep, and even now, his eyes fluttered open but quickly shut again. She gently rocked back and forth in the chair. These moments were precious to her. Too soon, he'd be too big for her to hold like this.

She continued rocking him for several more minutes until he was asleep. From the other room, she could hear Al shuffling around. She bit her lower lip. She'd been wanting to be alone with him ever since Aunt Betty had told her about Gilbert, and now was the perfect time.

She eased out of the chair and set the bottle down before tucking the boy into his bed. He let out a sigh of contentment and settled into a comfortable position. Pulling the blanket around his shoulders, she smiled and rubbed his back.

"You'll always have a home with me and your pa," she whispered.

He smiled in his sleep and she kissed his head.

She left the room and closed his door. When she reached her bedroom, she saw that Al hadn't gotten undressed yet. If she guessed right, he'd been searching for a hiding spot, somewhere he hoped she wouldn't find something. Maybe it was the gift he mentioned. He had mentioned going into town for some supplies, and he'd even brought some back. Maybe while he was at it, he got her the gift.

What a sweet man. He asked so little of others and yet gave so much. If anyone deserved the best, it was him. And while she wasn't as good as Hazel, she wanted to be the best she could be.

She entered the room and closed the door softly behind her. "It's taking you a long time to remove your clothes tonight. Do you need help?"

He chuckled and turned from a drawer he was shutting. "No, I can manage it on my own."

Closing the distance between them, she decided she wouldn't search the room and see if her gift was somewhere in here. In some ways, wondering what he got her was fun in itself. Just as he took off his shirt and undershirt, she took them from him and set them on the dresser. Then she wrapped her arms around his neck and kissed him.

"You're a wonderful man, Al," she said. "I'm glad you're my husband."

He brought his arms around her and smiled. "I am, too."

She kissed him again, but this time when it ended, she lowered her hands to his pants.

"Let me give you pleasure, Al," she whispered.

So he would understand her meaning, she unbuttoned his pants and slid her hands beneath his underwear so she could feel his erection. Had it been anyone but Al, she would have quickly let him go. But this was Al. It was his penis. It wasn't someone else's. And after all Al had done for her and for Gilbert, she wanted to do this.

When he placed his hands over hers to stop her from dropping his pants, she looked up at him. She loved him. This wouldn't be something she was doing for a customer. It'd be something she was doing for him, for her husband. And that made all the difference.

"I want to do this, Al. I understand we won't consummate the marriage yet, but I'd like to at least bring you to completion. Will you let me do that for you?"

He removed his hands and nodded.

She proceeded to take his pants off and then his underwear. After she encouraged him to sit on the bed, she knelt in front of him. He leaned slightly back, allowing her better access to him so she could wrap her hand around the base of his shaft. It took her a moment to get over the initial repulsion of the penis, but she glanced up at him and her stomach settled. This was Al. And she cared very much for him.

Returning her gaze to his erection, she brought her hand up to his tip then back down. She'd learned the rhythm long ago and quickly established it. She used to count as she did it to best distract her from what she was doing, but tonight, she didn't count. She just thought of Al finding Gilbert and raising him as his own. Never was a man more deserving of pleasure than her husband. Men needed sexual fulfillment. It was ingrained in them. And she wanted nothing more than to give this moment to him.

Leaning forward, she took him into her mouth, catching his slight intake of breath. Being a virgin, he wouldn't have known what it felt like to have a woman take him into her mouth, but now he did and she had no doubt it felt incredibly good to him. She traced her tongue over the slit in his tip and paused when she tasted the familiar saltiness from a bead of liquid that often preceded a man's climax. But she pressed forward and traced the rest of his tip. This was Al. She was doing this for him.

She had to keep reminding herself she was with Al as she continued her ministrations. And his moans helped. She was familiar with his voice. It comforted her. It enabled her to continue stroking him up and down his length as she teased his tip with her tongue. She knew he was close to release when he grew tense. She took a deep breath before she resumed what she'd started. It was for Al. Not someone else. Al would be the one receiving pleasure from what she was doing.

He climaxed in short time, and she accepted his seed into her mouth. For a split second she had to fight the urge to spit it out, only because this used to disgust her with the men who were particularly cruel to her. But Al was gentle and didn't shove himself deeper into her mouth. Once he was done, she swallowed and took a deep breath. He didn't smell the same as the other men, and his taste was different, too. That was good. These were things she could associate solely with him from now on.

She gently released him and glanced up at him, noting the soft smile on his lips. Despite the slight shaking in her hands, she returned his smile and sat next to him. It hadn't been harder than she feared it would be, but it'd taken a lot out of her to do this act, though she was glad she'd done it. Maybe next time, it would be easier.

He slipped his arm around her waist and kissed her neck. His action was so gentle it brought tears to her eyes. He loved her. He truly loved her. And he felt closer to her than he had before. She could feel it in the way he kissed her cheeks, her forehead, and then her lips.

"I want to give you pleasure, too," he whispered.

Surprised, she didn't know what to say at first. "Oh, well, I got pleasure out of giving you pleasure," she finally forced out. And it wasn't a lie. It'd satisfied her to know she pleased him instead of him having to take care of himself.

"I know, but I want to return the favor."

Before she could respond, he was unbuttoning her shirtwaist. She didn't want to tell him that it was pointless. No other man had been able to do it. Not even the ones who boasted they could make a woman orgasm two or three times in one night. She often thought they were lying but had no proof to make the accusation.

But she didn't have the heart to deny Al the right to try anyway. She didn't think she could ever deny him anything. So if he wanted to run his hands and mouth over her body and touch her intimately in hopes of bringing her pleasure, she'd let him. She'd even pretend he succeeded. She hadn't ever pretended such a thing with those men, but she'd pretend for Al. For him, it wasn't a challenge to prove his sexual prowess. It was a desire to do something for her.

She removed her clothes and settled back on the bed, fully expecting his hands to go immediately to her breasts or between her legs. But instead, he brought his mouth to hers and kissed her, not seeming to be in any hurry. He brought her into his arms and deepened the kiss. She opened her eyes at one point, just to reassure herself she was with Al. Relieved, she closed her eyes again to enjoy this part of what he was doing. His mouth left hers and he showered her with kisses on her cheeks and forehead again. This was nice. Much like his other kisses, but only better because this struck her as an act of devotion.

At one point, he lifted his head. She opened her eyes and turned her face toward him. "What is it?"

"Well, I..." He let out a light chuckle. "I don't think I'm going to be as good as you. I mean, you knew how to do everything. Just now." He cleared his throat. "Um, I was wondering where you'd like me to touch you."

No man had ever confessed he didn't know what to do. She brought her hand to his and clasped it. For a moment, she wasn't sure what to say since she'd never gotten any pleasure, but the men had seemed intent on touching her between her legs so she guided him to that area. Though he'd touched her here before, her face warmed. This was different from the other times he'd touched her. This time he was doing it for a purpose.

His fingers brushed her, light as a feather. She released her breath and relaxed. She glanced at the top of the drapes but then stopped herself. No. She wasn't with one of her customers. She was with Al. She needed to focus on him to remember that. Forcing her gaze back to him, she was relieved to note he was looking at the area between her legs where his hand was. That made it easier to watch him as he continued to explore her.

He was always gentle with her, and this time was no different. She figured she should let out a soft moan, something similar to what he'd done when she began stroking him. But then she realized what he was doing felt good. It startled her for a moment that she was even capable of the sensation. Then she relaxed again and opened herself up to it.

He slid a finger into her. "Is that alright?"

She nodded then realized his gaze was still on what his hand was doing. Clearing her throat, she said, "Yes, that's fine."

It didn't hurt. And in some small way, it was a pleasant feeling. She took a deep breath and forced her attention on the way his fingers felt as they continued to explore her. With him, it was different. Very much so, in fact. He lowered his head to her nearest breast and ran his tongue along her nipple. The action was just as gentle as everything else he was doing, except it caused a pleasant tingle to course through her.

"I like that," she whispered in surprise.

He continued teasing her nipple, choosing to start on the outside then work his way in before lightly sucking it. A soft moan escaped her throat—this one real—and she became aware of a heated wetness settling between her legs. Had she not become aware of the pressure beginning to well up in her core, she might have cried from the way he tenderly touched her.

Her hands slid up and down his back at a slow, methodical pace, giving her a chance to familiarize herself with the way he felt. He was strong but he never used his strength against her. He used it to protect, and she was safe with him. She didn't have to constantly watch what she said or worry that he might strike her in a moment of anger.

His thumb brushed her sensitive nub and she gasped from the spark of pleasure that centered in on that region of her body.

He lifted his head and looked at her. "Did I hurt you?"

"No," she whispered. "I liked it."

She didn't dare say how much. She had never liked it when the other men had touched her there, but with him, she wanted more of it. Bringing his hand back to her curls, she encouraged him to slide two fingers into her. That action alone caused her to moan again. But her attention went to his thumb and she pressed it against her nub. It took her some time to figure out the exact way she wanted him to caress her.

When she did figure it out, however, she fully gave herself over to the wave of sensations his stroking produced. She let go of his hand and grasped his arm. It was wonderful. Simply wonderful. She had no idea her body was capable of such pleasure. Was this how it'd been for him when she'd taken him into her mouth? If so, then her only regret was that she hadn't done it for him sooner, hadn't insisted they do something for him—even if he didn't want to consummate the marriage.

"Is that alright?" he asked, his voice hinting that he wasn't sure he was pleasing her.

"Yes," she rasped, lifting her hips and taking his fingers deeper into her. Even that part of his stroking felt wonderful. For certain, it was more intense than before. "Don't stop."

"I won't," he promised then brought his mouth back to her breast.

She closed her eyes, still aware of the way he felt as she rubbed his back. She could smell the soap he used to wash his hair. She felt his body pressed next to hers. Everything was him and it only heightened her pleasure. Soon her hips were rocking in rhythm to his ministrations, the pressure in her core demanding she keep going, that she find out what a climax was like.

She murmured his name, another reminder that he was the one doing this for her. But in due time, her focus went solely to the mounting pressure and she let out a cry as she found her release. She held onto him, absorbing each wave of pleasure as it swept over her. After several moments passed, her body relaxed and she let out a sigh of contentment. She'd never felt so good in her life.

Al lifted his head and looked at her, and she caught the question in his eyes.

"Yes," she whispered, still out of breath. "You gave me pleasure."

He smiled and brought her into his arms. "I thought I did, but it's nice to be sure." He kissed her. "I want to satisfy you."

"You did."

She wrapped her arms around his waist and snuggled up to him. She had no idea that she could experience joy after being intimate with a man, but Al was quickly showing her that things she didn't believe possible were possible after all. She brought her mouth to his and kissed him again. She thought to ask him if he wanted to consummate the marriage tonight but thought better of it. They had both given each other pleasure and for now, that was enough. They would do more in the future.

When she ended the kiss, she rested her head on his shoulder, and in time, they both fell asleep.

Chapter Twelve

When Sadie woke up the next morning, she was surprised she was alone in bed. She fully expected Al to want to finally consummate their marriage now that they had both given and received pleasure the previous night. She got out of bed, washed up, and dressed. By the time she finished tying her hair back with a ribbon, the bedroom door opened.

A smile crossed her face when she saw Al carrying a tray with a plate of eggs and pancakes on it. "Are you bringing me breakfast in bed?" she asked, pleased he'd do something like that for her.

"I was hoping to surprise you."

"I am surprised."

"Yes, but I wanted to kiss you while you still slept and then present you with breakfast."

She closed the distance between them and kissed him. "It's a wonderful surprise, Al. I doubt other husbands are so thoughtful."

He grinned. "Well, since you're already up, you might as well come out here."

She wrapped her arm around his and walked with him to the table. "It'll be better this way. I'd like to eat with you."

He set the tray on the table then turned to her and brought her into his arms. "At some point, I still want to serve you breakfast in bed."

"Tomorrow morning, I'll linger in bed a little longer so you have time to do it."

"Deal." He pulled out the chair for her. "Since I already made breakfast, I want you to sit down. I'll take care of everything."

"You shouldn't go through such a fuss over me," she replied, hesitant to sit.

He took her hand and led her to the chair. "I won't be doing this all the time. Believe me, there will be days when I can barely find time to shave. But there are those rare days where all the animals are doing well and Gilbert's still asleep. Days like this don't come often. You got to make the most of them."

Returning his smile, she squeezed his hand. "Alright."

She sat down and he pushed the chair in. She thought he would go over to the stove and bring his meal over, but he placed his hands on her shoulders and kissed her neck. Her body warmed with pleasure.

As he turned his attention to setting the table, she folded her hands in her lap. "Is there anything you want to do today?"

"I thought I'd let Aunt Betty watch Gilbert today so you and I can go to town. We can make a day of it, you know? Eat at the restaurant, do a little shopping, take in a nice walk. It won't be long before enough snow comes and we'll be stuck here." Shooting her a teasing grin, he added, "You might want to pick up a dime novel or two to read. It's likely to get boring around here with it just being me and Gilbert for company."

Laughing at his joke, she waved her hand dismissively at him. "You and Gilbert are a delight."

"Even when my clothes get all muddy and Gilbert drools all over himself? I seem to remember you having your hands full of laundry the other day."

"I don't mind doing laundry," she assured him as he sat across from her.

He picked up his fork and leaned forward, his eyes twinkling. "Just wait until we have a couple more children and you're up to your elbows in dirty clothes. Aunt Betty says there's no end in sight for a mother when it comes to dirty clothes."

"I can think of worse things for a woman to do with her time," she replied then lowered her gaze to the plate full of pancakes and eggs in front of her. She'd much rather do laundry for him and all of their children than be back at that godforsaken brothel. "I love being here, Al." She looked back at him. "It's more wonderful than I dared hope when I came here."

"I'm glad to hear that, Hazel."

Her smile faltered a bit but then she forced it back. Turning her attention to her plate, she ate her meal.

When they were done, she took care of Gilbert while Al cared for the animals. The process went smoothly, and they were soon on their way to Aunt Betty and Bear's.

"Are you sure they won't mind?" Sadie asked as Al turned the wagon up the path that led to their friends' cabin.

"I'm sure." Shooting her a sly smile, he added, "I ran into Aunt Betty yesterday while I was in town and asked if she would watch Gilbert so we could have the day together. But I told her I had to make sure it was alright with you first."

Sadie relaxed. She hated to come by unannounced. Aunt Betty had been so nice to them already. "How long have you known Aunt Betty and her husband?"

"Ever since I got here three years ago. I came up for the free land that was being offered."

"Where did you come from?"

"Minnesota. My dad was a farmer."

She didn't know why she hadn't thought to ask about his parents before, but now she was intrigued about his past. "Are they still alive?"

He shook his head. "Afraid not. Both got sick during a bad winter and died. I was fifteen at the time. My parents were immigrants and had me in this country so I never met any of my relatives. When my parents died and the land went to someone else, I left and did odd jobs here and there for a lot of years. I spent most of the time working on railways. Then I came here." He shrugged. "This place grew on me and I decided to make my home here."

"I bet it's nothing like Minnesota."

"It's not. But that's what makes it nice. I like the hills and the trees."

"I do, too."

"So, what about you? What made you decide to come all the way up here?"

She should have known that by asking him about his past, he'd start asking about hers. Clearing her throat, she turned her attention to Gilbert, pretending to fuss over the hood of his coat. "Oh, there's not much to tell, really. Everything that was interesting, I already told you in the letters."

"All you said was that your father was a plantation owner who almost lost everything after the Civil War. Through careful planning, he managed to hold onto his wealth. But you said none of that mattered to you. You said all you wanted was a quiet little place where you could have peace. I often wondered about that, but I guess it had to do with the war. That must have been hard to experience."

Sadie hadn't thought about Hazel being around to see the effects of the war. She knew so little about the woman's life, and yet she couldn't deny the connection she felt to her. Had she the chance to know her, Sadie had no doubt they would have been good friends.

She smiled at Al. "I do like how peaceful it is out here. I'm happier than I've ever been."

"I'm glad to hear it," he replied.

They reached Aunt Betty's and he pulled the brake. Relieved for the reprieve from having to try to dodge questions about Atlanta, she talked to Aunt Betty for a few minutes. Once she and Al were on their way to town, he scooted closer to her and wrapped his arm around her shoulders.

"I wanted to do this on the first day you came here," he admitted and kissed her cheek.

"Why didn't you?" she asked, unable to keep the teasing tone out of her voice.

"I was too shy. It was like a dream. I couldn't believe that someone as beautiful as you would marry me."

"Why was that so hard to believe? You're a handsome man." Noting the pleased expression on his face, she giggled and kissed his cheek. "Why don't you think you're good looking?"

"I'm...adequate."

"You're more than adequate. You're absolutely wonderful." Since his face grew red, she studied him and smiled. He was blushing. "Al, you have no need to be so shy with me. Surely, you must know that I adore you more and more each day."

He pulled back the reins so the horses stopped. His gaze met hers. "I love you."

"I love you, too."

He cupped the side of her face in his hand and lowered his head. His lips brushed hers, light at first but then his mouth parted, an indication he wanted to deepen the kiss. She slipped her arms around his neck and pulled him closer to her. She'd never kissed a man in a wooded area. The smells from the trees, the hint of fall in the air, the cool air around them. She'd experienced none of this before while with a man. This was all new to her. And since it was new, it was something she wanted to explore. There was no better place to make love.

Before she had time to think through her next move, she unbuttoned his pants. If he didn't think about it, maybe he'd finally consummate their marriage. She wanted to do this. She wanted to do this in the secluded area, surrounded by nothing but trees and the blue sky above them.

"Make love to me, Al," she whispered. "Make me your wife. Please?"

"Are you sure?" he asked, even as she knew his erection had to be pressing him to do as she requested.

Her gaze went to his and she noted the glimmer of hope in his eyes. He wanted to be intimate with her, had wanted it from the time they got married. But even while he'd wanted it, he held back for her sake. He loved her. She mattered to him. It wouldn't be a quick and meaningless act. It would draw him closer to her, and she wanted that more than she wanted anything.

"I'm sure, Al," she whispered. "I've never been more sure of anything in my life."

With a nod, he cast aside the rest of his hesitation and set the brake on the wagon. He brought her back into his arms and kissed her again, this time his kisses more urgent than before. And he didn't just kiss her on the mouth. He sprinkled kisses on her cheeks, her chin, and her neck. No one had ever showered her with such affection, and this made it easy to get caught up in the surge of his passion.

She helped him take off her coat, shirtwaist and chemise so he could explore her breasts. He was gentle as he caressed them, his touch tentative as he cupped them then ran his thumbs along her nipples. She closed her eyes for a moment, enjoying the way he kissed her neck while he continued his ministrations. The air was cool on her skin, but his hands were warm. She liked the contrast. It was something she hadn't experienced before. It was something she could connect with him—and only him. Opening her eyes, she took in the trees around them. The place was a private one, affording them both the freedom to be together without the risk of being caught. But more than that, she loved the smell. Clean, fresh, earthy.

Turning her attention back to him, she encouraged him to lower his trousers and underwear. She lifted her skirt and straddled him. He wrapped her in a protective embrace and kissed her neck. It was so much like him. All of his movements—the way he kissed and touched her—spoke of tenderness and love, something she had never shared with any of the other men. And that was new, too. It was something else to connect solely with him. She shifted until he was intimately snuggled against the slit in her bloomers.

Recalling the way he'd made her feel the night before when he stroked her sensitive nub, she slid against his shaft, delighted when she experienced the same spark of pleasure as it brushed against him. Ordinarily, she'd take the man inside her, but with Al, she wanted to slow down and enjoy what they were doing. He continued kissing her neck, murmuring for her to rub against him again as he placed his hands on her hips and guided her movements. She soon established a rhythm that brought her closer to the same peak she'd had the night before. Now that she knew what to expect, she had something she could work toward. And it wasn't long before she climaxed, her movements coming to a stop and her breathing shallow as her core clenched and unclenched in time to the waves of pleasure that engulfed her.

When she relaxed, he shifted beneath her and centered his tip at her entrance. Biting her lower lip, she drew him closer until he entered her. She let out a sigh, surprised it felt as good as it did. He let out a low moan and kissed her again. His tongue brushed hers before he began the all-too-familiar rhythm of rocking his hips.

She held onto him and worked with him, glad they were doing this in a place she'd never done it before. It helped her remember she wasn't servicing a customer. Her husband—the man she loved who loved her in return—was making love to her. It wasn't a cold transaction. It meant something. And afterwards, he wouldn't be giving her money and leaving only to return when he wanted her to satisfy his carnal needs again.

She kept repeating his name inside her mind, doing everything possible to sear this new experience into her memory so she wouldn't remember the others that had come before him. And in time, she was able to focus on him.

He stilled and moaned, signaling his release. She held him closer to her and kissed his neck. After he relaxed, she remained connected to him. In the past, she'd gotten off the men as soon as possible and wiped their seed off of her to scrub away their scent. But she didn't want to lose Al's scent. In a way, he had claimed her, marked her as his. And she would never have anyone else but him again.

Al cupped her face in his hands and kissed her, this time gently, his former passion now given way to contentment. "That was worth the wait," he whispered, a smile on his face.

"Was it?" she asked, unable to stop her own smile as she took in his joy.

He nodded. "I knew it'd be best when the timing was right." He brought her hands to his lips and kissed them.

She'd never experienced such an act of devotion and had to swallow back the lump in her throat so she wouldn't break down and cry. Never in her entire life did she think making love could be like this, that it was more than about physical release. But now she knew better and it was all because of him.

"We'd better get to town before it gets too late," he said and gave her hips a playful squeeze.

"Alright," she replied and wiggled off of him. "I don't want to miss the opportunity to get you something special for Christmas."

"You decided you're getting me something?"

Noting the pleased tone in his voice, she slipped on her chemise and shirtwaist while he buttoned up his pants. "Of course, I'm getting you something. Besides, what else did you think I was going to do with the money you gave me?"

He tucked in his shirt. "I thought you'd get something you wanted."

"And I want to give you a gift."

She finished buttoning her shirtwaist, and he helped her into her coat. He gave her a smile and kissed her. "I used to go to Aunt Betty and Bear's to celebrate Christmas when the weather was good enough. Don't get me wrong. I enjoyed it. But I'm looking forward to celebrating it with you and Gilbert."

"I'm looking forward to it, too."

He leaned forward and released the brake. She slipped her arm around his and settled her head on his shoulder as he continued their trek to town.

Chapter Thirteen

Sadie picked up the belt buckle in the mercantile and inspected it. It was beautiful. The image on the golden oval was of the trees. She ran her thumb along the smooth metal. It would be perfect for Al. She had no idea how to put it on a belt, but she thought Aunt Betty would show her what to do. She checked the price and saw she had just enough to buy it.

Looking over at the mercantile owner, she saw he was done with the customer he'd been helping. She glanced out the small window, relieved when she saw that Al was still outside. He promised to wait for her to buy his gift before he came in to look for something they could get Gilbert. She wouldn't have blamed him for sneaking into the mercantile to take a peek at what she was buying. It wasn't easy to resist looking for her gift.

After she made the purchase, she stepped out of the mercantile and hurried over to the wagon. With a teasing grin, he gestured to the package in her hands. "I take it your mission was a success."

"It was," she replied. "Want a hint?"

"No."

"No?"

"I want to be surprised when I see it," he said as he took the package from her and tucked it away under her seat.

She grinned. "I can't help but notice you're holding on to that package longer than necessary."

He glanced over at her and chuckled. "No, I'm not."

"You are, too. But it won't do you any good. I had the mercantile owner wrap it with some extra paper so you can't tell what it is by feeling it."

"Alright. Maybe I wanted a little hint. You can't blame a man for being curious."

Laughing, she accepted his arm and walked with him back to the mercantile. "No, I can't. But don't you dare try to wiggle a hint from the owner."

"I won't. I promise I'll be on my best behavior."

"Thank you."

They entered the store and the owner's eyebrows rose. "Did you wish to return the object?" he called out.

"Not at all," she replied. "Now that I bought my husband his Christmas present, we can buy other items in your fine store."

"I certainly don't mind people coming back to buy more things," the owner said. "By all means, you can return as many times as you want."

"Will do," Al replied.

Sadie turned to a couple of wooden toys. "Which one do you think Gilbert will like best?"

"I don't know."

"Well, what did you like when you were a boy?"

"I don't recall much about what I did when I was a child other than follow my pa all over the farm."

"Oh come now. Surely, there must be something you remember."

"I remember banging on the milk pail and singing." When she waited for him to add more, he shrugged. "Sorry. That's all I got. I don't think I had any toys."

"I wish I knew more about what children like. I should have paid more attention to the things at Aunt Betty's house. I bet she has some toys."

He patted the small of her back. "We'll get him the wooden horse and rider."

"That's good." She picked the items up and studied them. "He can pretend it's you on one of your horses."

"He might be a little young to pretend that."

"Maybe. You're probably right."

"But when he gets older, he will."

She smiled and headed over to the counter so they could make the purchase, but he stopped her and gestured to the shelf along the wall.

"Are you sure you don't want to pick up a couple of dime novels?" he asked.

"No. I have everything I want."

"Oh. I suppose you'd rather read other books. You probably read literary works instead of dime novels growing up. I could stop by Aunt Betty's and see if she has any."

"No, that's alright. To be honest, I don't read books."

"Did you want something else to do to help pass the time?" he offered.

"Well..." She scanned the store, not sure what to take.

"Winter's a long time. We'll probably be stuck for at least three months in the cabin."

"I wouldn't mind doing some sewing," she decided. "I know Aunt Betty has given us everything we need, but I do find it soothing to work on something."

"Let's get you some things to sew then."

As he led her over to the cloths, buttons, ribbons, and other items she could use, she couldn't help but say, "I take it your gift for me doesn't include anything to sew."

He opened his mouth to answer her but then stopped and laughed. "You're a sly one. Trying to wiggle out a hint."

"But it must be true since you so easily agreed to let me pick out anything I want in this area."

"Alright. You win. Yes, it has nothing to do with sewing. But that is the only hint you'll get from me."

"It's good enough," she assured him.

After she selected the things she wanted, they bought the items, and he set the crate in the back of the wagon. Then he took her to a restaurant that was smaller than the ones she was used to in Omaha. Her mind flashed back to the day her life changed, when Hazel had granted her the gift of freedom. Even now, her gaze went to the back corner of the place. Three old men were sitting at the table, laughing and talking as they ate their lunch. There was no lone woman, huddled in hopes no one would notice her.

Sadie's eyebrows furrowed. Had Hazel been frightened? Had she been running from someone? Something about her had drawn Sadie to her. Perhaps Hazel had been a prisoner, much like herself. Except Hazel's prison wasn't a brothel. It'd been something else. She swallowed and blinked back her tears. How she wished she had asked Hazel what made her answer a mail-order bride ad. But at the time, she was so frightened by the blood Hazel kept coughing up, it never occurred to her to ask her about her past.

"Sweetheart," a gentle voice whispered in her ear.

Sadie turned to Al. "I'm sorry. I was thinking of what your gift might be."

He chuckled. "Why do I have the feeling that you're not going to give up on trying to figure out what your gift is until you actually open it?"

Glad he bought her lie, she smiled and shrugged. "Because I can't help but be curious when I know there's something good waiting for me?"

"Well, right now you have lunch to look forward to. Come. Let's sit."

She was relieved when he picked a place away from the corner of the room. This was supposed to be a pleasant day.

Al handed her the menu.

She lowered her gaze and glanced at the letters that had no meaning to her. "I'll have whatever you are."

"Are you sure? I might order something disgusting."

"No, you won't," she replied, amused. "You always make good food."

"Alright. Let's see." He read through the menu and asked, "How does pot roast with mashed potatoes sound?"

"Sounds wonderful. I couldn't have done better myself."

The waitress came over to them, and he ordered their meals. Despite Sadie's better judgment, she glanced over her shoulder, her mind unwittingly going back to Hazel. Yes, she had many questions about Hazel, but they'd never be answered. Hazel died and when she did, all the answers died with her. The only thing that Sadie could do was be thankful Hazel had given her another chance at life.

She looked at Al and smiled. Hazel had done so much for her. Yes. The best way to honor her memory was to embrace the gift Hazel had given her. And that was exactly what she'd do.

***

Late that afternoon when Sadie and Al arrived at Aunt Betty and Bear's, Al helped her down from the wagon and gave her a lingering kiss.

"What was that for?" she asked.

"For giving me the best day of my life," he replied.

"It was wonderful for me, too."

"That's what makes it so perfect."

He kissed her again then took her hand and led her to the cabin. Though the air was cooler than before, her skin was still warm from the kiss he'd given her.

They went up the porch steps, and just before he could knock on the door, a girl opened it. "I thought I saw you come up the road."

"You did," Al replied and patted her shoulder. "I hope Gilbert didn't give your ma too much trouble."

"He was an angel the whole time you were gone," Aunt Betty called out. "He's an easy baby."

"Thank you for watching him," Sadie told her as she went over to pick him up from the floor where he was playing with some wooden blocks. "Hey, sweetie. Did you miss me?"

Gilbert wrapped his arms around her neck and gave her a hug.

Smiling, she kissed his head and rubbed his back. "I missed you, too," she whispered. And she had. While she enjoyed her day with Al, it felt good to return to Gilbert.

"No one can take a mother's place," Aunt Betty told her.

Glancing at Al to make sure he wasn't in hearing distance, she lowered her voice. "I got Al his gift today for Christmas. It's a belt buckle, but I don't know how to put it on his belt."

"I can help you with that, and I have a leather strap we can make into a belt."

"Oh. I didn't think of making a new belt."

"Well, if he sees his old one missing, he might figure out what you're doing." She winked at her. "Don't you worry. We got plenty of leather around here, thanks to the animals Al helps us catch."

"Aunt Betty," Sadie began, hesitant to ask but figuring it was a safe question to ask since Hazel wouldn't already know the answer, "why does Al refer to you as 'Aunt' Betty but he doesn't refer to Bear as 'Uncle' Bear?"

The woman laughed. "When Al first came here, he reminded me so much of one of my nephews. I couldn't help but take him in as a member of my family. Bear says being called

'Uncle' makes him feel old and he'd rather think of Al as a friend instead of a young kid."

Sadie thought it seemed so much like Aunt Betty to take everyone under her wing and care for them as a mother hen. "You're a sweet woman." On impulse, she hugged her. "Thank you for everything you do for me and Al."

"I'm happy to do it."

"I'm still learning how to cook and sew, but if you ever need anything, I hope you don't hesitate to ask."

"The offer is much appreciated, Hazel."

It took Sadie a moment to remember everyone thought she was Hazel. She returned Aunt Betty's smile. It was easy to forget that she wasn't really Hazel, especially on days as lovely as this one.

Her gaze went to Al who was talking to Bear by the front door. She'd made love to him as Sadie, not Hazel. She'd laughed and talked to him as Sadie, not Hazel. And she'd come to Aunt Betty with her request about the belt buckle as Sadie, not Hazel. So many things she'd done with them since she arrived in Rapid City, she'd done as herself. That meant they liked her for her, not because of who they thought she was. Didn't it?

Rubbing Gilbert's back, Sadie thanked Aunt Betty again, and they went over to Al and Bear.

"Talking about my gift?" Al asked, his eyes twinkling.

"As a matter of fact, we were," Sadie replied, glad for the reprieve from thinking about Hazel. "She said she'd come over and help me with it."

His eyebrows furrowed, and she took a small bit of delight in knowing she had confused him about what it could be.

"I'll come by in a couple days," Aunt Betty said.

"That sounds good," she replied.

"Bear and I were talking about hunting tomorrow," Al told Sadie. "They could use another good deer or elk for the winter."

Sadie nodded. "I think that's a wonderful idea."

A round of giggling caught their attention, and Sadie looked out the doorway in time to see Missy with her little brother and sister following her. All carried buckets of water.

"You're all acting like a bunch of babies," Missy admonished, not amused by whatever antics the other two were pulling.

Sadie wondered where the other sister was and saw her walking around the coop by the barn, feeding the hens.

"We're just having fun," Missy's younger sister said.

"No," Missy replied with a heavy sigh, "you're not. You're being irresponsible. You can't keep tossing buckets of water on the ground so I lose count of how many I filled up."

"Where's your sense of humor?" the brother asked.

"Just carry your buckets," Missy said in irritation.

They came to the porch and the adults moved aside so they could enter the cabin.

"There's never a dull moment around here," Aunt Betty commented with a chuckle.

Bear winked at Al and Sadie. "Just you two wait until Gilbert's older and has little brothers and sisters to contend with."

Al glanced at Sadie and smiled. "We're looking forward to it, chaos and all."

Sadie's face grew warm from his meaning. She'd love nothing more than to have his children.

"I'm sure Gilbert will like having a brother or sister to play with," Aunt Betty chimed in.

"Are you kidding?" Missy asked as she set the pails down. "I wish I was an only kid."

"You would have gotten bored if it'd just been you," Aunt Betty replied with a wave of her hand then turned to Sadie. "Don't let her deter you from having a house full of children. A big house is a happy house, even if there are times when they fight."

"I don't know," Bear argued as he stroked his chin. "Sometimes I miss the quiet."

"That's why you go hunting," she told him with a pointed look.

"That's true." He gave Al a nod. "See you bright and early."

Al slipped his arm around Sadie's waist to lead her down the porch steps. They made it to the third step when the youngest girl let out an ear-piercing scream, followed by the boy's laughter.

"Go on and chop some wood since you're so bored you're pulling on your sister's hair," Bear told the laughing boy.

"I think it's best if we don't look back," Al whispered and continued to lead her to their wagon.

Chuckling, Sadie decided he was right. In due time, they'd have to deal with their own children who'd do the same kinds of things. She looked down at Gilbert who was smiling and babbling in her arms. It was hard to believe he'd ever argue with his brothers and sisters. He was such a happy child.

They reached the wagon and he helped her into it. Once he was settled beside her, she placed Gilbert on her lap. "You really don't think Gilbert will pick on his little brothers or sisters, do you?" she asked.

He released the brake and grinned. "Yes, I do. Children are children. They're going to do what they will. All we can do is send them out to do chores so they have better things to do than argue with each other." He kissed her cheek. "Disappointed?"

"No. It's just hard to believe, that's all. He's a happy boy, don't you think?"

"Yes, he is happy, and even when he argues with his brothers and sisters, he can still be happy." He shrugged. "At least when they make up, they'll be friends again."

"They will be friends."

"They'll play together a lot. I've seen Aunt Betty and Bear's children when they're getting along. Don't worry. Gilbert and his brothers and sisters will have a lot of fun growing up together."

"You're right." She turned her attention back to Gilbert as Al led the horses down the path. "They will." She smiled and thought about all the good times waiting for him.

Chapter Fourteen

On Christmas morning, Sadie woke up to a big hug from Al. Eyes still closed, she smiled as he kissed her cheek. "Good morning, sweetheart," he whispered.

"It is good," she murmured. Every morning she woke up in this quaint cabin was a good one.

He slid his arm around her waist and snuggled against her. "Today you get to open your gift."

"I think you're more excited about it than I am."

"I probably am, but I think you'll like it."

He nuzzled her neck and she giggled. She was quickly learning that Al had a playful side to him. "You're a lot of fun to be around."

"I'm glad you think so. It'd be horrible if you thought I was boring."

"No, I'd never think that. You're anything but boring."

"Good." He released her and pulled off her blanket. "Come on. I can't wait anymore. I want you to see what I got you."

Chuckling, she sat up. "I bet I can't even talk you into lingering in bed if I promise you wonderful pleasures?"

"Not this morning." He picked her up and set her on her feet.

Amused, she watched as he retrieved her robe and slipped it over her shoulders. "You're not even going to wait until I get dressed?" she asked.

"You can get dressed afterwards."

"This must be good."

He kissed her. "It is."

Intrigued, she followed him out of the bedroom. "Are we going to get Gilbert up?"

"Not yet. I want you to open your gift first."

He hurried over to the small tree he placed in the corner of the living area and waved for her to come join him.

Her smile widened as she crossed the room and sat next to him. "I'm surprised you were able to wait until Christmas for me to open it." She accepted the small box wrapped in brown paper and shook it. "I don't hear anything."

"You're not supposed to because I protected it."

Eyebrows raised, she asked, "Protect it? Is it fragile?"

"Open it and see."

"Alright. I think the suspense is going to kill you," she teased.

She proceeded to open the gift, and though she knew it was sneaky, she intentionally took her time. When she got to the box, she lifted the lid and stared at the ring with a gold band and a perfectly sculpted pink rose on it with two green leaves on either side.

"The man I bought it from said he mixed silver and copper to get the pink and green coloring in the design," Al told her. "I ordered it right after we got married."

"It's beautiful," she whispered, tracing the ring with her thumb.

"I thought you'd like it. Aunt Betty says that every bride should have a ring." He gestured to it. "Put it on."

She did and smiled when she realized it fit perfectly.

"I was hoping I was right when I estimated your ring size," he said. "You have no idea how hard it was to not take the ring out and make sure I guessed right."

"You did a wonderful job," she replied and kissed him. "Thank you, Al. It's a lovely gift."

"When you look at it, you can think of us."

"I will. And I love it." Especially the reason he got it. No wonder he was so excited about it.

"Can I open my gift?" he asked.

"Of course, you can." She retrieved it from under the tree and gave it to him. "I don't think it's as good as the one you got me."

"Nonsense. It will be because you were thinking of me when you got it."

"Well, to be fair, Aunt Betty helped me with it," she said as he tore into the paper. She nudged him in the side and laughed. "Are you that impatient to see what it is?"

He shot her an amused look. "I don't see the point in taking forever to unwrap the paper like you do."

"I like the suspense of waiting to see what it is."

"I guess so. I think it took you an entire minute to unwrap my gift. And that was a small one."

She shook her head but didn't protest as he finished ripping into the brown paper. When he pulled out the brown leather belt with the gold buckle on it, she said, "I had Aunt Betty's help in tanning the belt and then attaching the buckle to it."

"It's great. Thank you."

He leaned toward her and kissed her, bringing her into his arms. In the short time she'd been Al's wife, she'd discovered how pleasant it could be to be intimate with a man. She had no idea kissing didn't always have to lead to the bedroom. She also had no idea that the bedroom was something she could look forward to. She thought it was solely for the man's pleasure, but she'd come to discover it was also for the woman's pleasure. With Al, all things were new, and it was like the past never happened. In many ways, it was like a fairytale where all her dreams came true.

When he ended the kiss, he gave her waist a gentle squeeze. "Are you ready to get Gilbert up so he can open his gift?"

She nodded and helped him to his feet. They went to his room and she softly opened the door and saw Gilbert was stirring in the crib. "I think he's ready to get up," she whispered and crossed the small room. She rubbed the boy's belly, and his gaze went to her. A smile lit up his face and she picked him up. "You're such a happy thing, aren't you?" She glanced at Al who was getting a cloth diaper ready on the small table. "If we have another baby, do you think he or she will be as good-natured as Gilbert?"

Al shrugged. "I don't know if all babies are like him or if it's just who he is. Aunt Betty says some people are born looking for the best in everything and others seem to be skeptical as soon as they come into the world. Even in the same family, you get kids who are different."

She placed Gilbert on the table, pulled off his clothes and started with the process of changing his diaper. "When will Gilbert be one?"

"Well," Al leaned against the wall and crossed his arms, "I found him on March 19. Aunt Betty guessed he was born right around that time, judging by how small he was."

"You have no idea who his parents are?"

"Nope. I didn't see anyone around the area, and I didn't know if a woman in town had been expecting a child. But then I don't go to town during the winter months and pretty much keep to myself."

"Aunt Betty didn't have any ideas?"

"Her best guess is that it was someone traveling through the area," he replied.

Sadie finished pinning the new diaper on Gilbert who was squirming around and giggling. She glanced at Al. "Do you want to celebrate his birthday on the day you found him?"

"Yes. I think it fits close enough to when he was actually born."

She sat Gilbert on the table and put on the day clothes Aunt Betty had given them. "It works. March 19 is a good day to celebrate his birthday." After a moment, she asked, "Do you plan to tell him the truth? About how you found him and all?"

"I'll have to. I don't think it'll be easy for him, but I think telling him the truth will be best."

"Maybe."

"You don't think it's a good idea?"

"I'm not sure what the best thing to do is," she admitted as she buttoned Gilbert's clothes. "It's bound to be painful when he discovers his parents abandoned him."

"Probably, but it might be worse if we led him to believe you had him and he finds out later on we lied to him."

"Is it really a lie if you don't tell him anything at all?"

"Yes, not telling him anything would still be a lie."

She picked Gilbert up and he wrapped his arms around her neck. She hesitated to say anything else, especially in light of the enjoyable morning they'd shared, but she had to ask, "What if you told a lie because you knew the person wouldn't like the truth? What if you knew that person would hate you if you told them?"

"I don't see why Gilbert would hate us when we tell him the truth. Sure, he'll be hurt to learn his real parents left him, but I think he'll be glad we took him in and raised him as our own."

He missed the point of her question. She'd been asking about lying in general, but he assumed she was still talking about

Gilbert. And she didn't have the courage to clarify what she'd meant.

He kissed her. "It'll work out. He won't hate us. We'll tell him when he's old enough to understand the situation." He patted the small of her back. "Come on. Let's show him his present."

Sadie had no doubt that Gilbert would understand when he learned the truth. Sure, he'd be hurt, but he'd also realize that she and Al loved him. But from time to time, she wondered if Al would—or even could—love her if he knew she wasn't really Hazel. He had such a high standard on what was right and wrong. She didn't think he'd understand why she lied.

She made her decision back in Omaha to be Hazel, and that was something she'd live with until the day she died. But did it really matter? She was her real self with Al. She might be able to assume a different name with a shadowy past, but that was all she was doing. When it came down to her day-to-day actions, she was her real self. That was the important thing. And she loved him. There was no deception in any of that.

Deciding to let the matter go, she went to the tree and sat down, setting Gilbert on her lap. Al sat next to her and retrieved the two gifts for him.

"This is from me and your ma," Al said, holding them out to the boy.

Gilbert took them and put one in his mouth.

"You're not supposed to eat it, silly," Sadie protested, laughing as she took it out of his mouth. "You're supposed to open it to see what's under all this paper." She demonstrated by carefully ripping a small piece of the paper apart. She handed it back to him. "There. Now you do it."

Gilbert tore apart the paper in a hurry and almost flung the wooden horse across the room, but Al caught it. "You're pretty strong there, boy," Al said. "You'll need that strength for chopping wood when you get older."

She rubbed Gilbert's back as he leaned forward and hurried to open his other gift. "He's already gotten so big since I came here. When Aunt Betty said babies don't stay babies for long, she wasn't kidding."

"Bear said it was good they don't stay little for long. He said he was relieved when he no longer had to worry about changing diapers."

"He? I don't recall hearing that he ever changed a diaper."

"Alright, it was Aunt Betty who did all that, but he remembered the way the cabin smelled." Al scooted closer to her and wrapped his arm around her shoulders. "Did I ever tell you that I'm glad you change the diapers now?"

She grinned. "No, but I figured it out when you started bolting out of the cabin whenever Gilbert needed a new one."

"I don't bolt out of the cabin when he needs a new one."

She shot him a pointed look.

"Well, not every time," he clarified.

"Setting a new one on the table isn't the same as doing the whole thing. But," she added and kissed him, "I have no desire to cut up and preserve animal meat. I'd much rather stand back and hand you things you need."

"We make a good team, don't we?"

"We do." She looked down at Gilbert and saw he was chewing on the wooden person. Taking it out of his mouth, she said, "That's not food. It's a toy."

Gilbert tossed aside his wooden toys and grabbed the paper which he then tore into smaller pieces.

Al chuckled. "I think we should have asked Aunt Betty what a child Gilbert's age should play with." He collected the wooden horse and man. "I'll put this away until he's older."

"I didn't think he'd try to teethe on them," Sadie said.

"I didn't either. But as Aunt Betty says, being a parent is a learning experience. We'll do better next time." Al kissed her then rubbed the boy's hair before he stood up with the toys. "I'll get breakfast this morning. You sit and watch Gilbert enjoy the paper."

"What about the animals?" she asked as he headed for their bedroom.

"I took care of them before I woke you up."

She wondered just how early he got up that morning. She had no idea anyone could get so excited about a present, but she had to admit the ring was the best gift she'd ever received. Taking a good look at it in the morning light that filtered through the window, she smiled. Every time she looked at it, she would think of him and the wonderful life they shared. This Christmas was the best one she'd ever had. And better yet, there would be more Christmases just like it in the future.

Chapter Fifteen

It was May when the stranger came. Al had just finished tending to his garden when he saw the man ride up to his property on a horse. From the looks of it, he was well-to-do, what with his fancy suit and all. The dust from town had gotten on his pants and shoes, but the man didn't seem to notice.

Al set down his hoe and hurried to meet him. "Are you lost?" he called out as he wiped his hands on his handkerchief.

The man scanned him up and down then smiled as if he was amused by something no one else saw but him. "That depends. Does Hazel McPherson live here?"

The man's gaze went to the cabin, and Al couldn't be sure, but he thought the man snickered. Shifting a bit, he tucked the handkerchief back into his back pocket. "She goes by Hazel Grover now."

The man looked back at him and his eyebrows rose. "Then I'm not lost." He got off the steed and handed Al the reins. "I'm Hazel's cousin. My name is James McPherson."

Al's eyebrows furrowed. Her cousin? But he had a different accent from Hazel. "Where do you live?"

"Atlanta, Georgia."

Yes, that was where Hazel was from, but he didn't sound anything like her. "All your life?"

He chuckled and nodded. "Yes. I gather she didn't tell you about me."

"No," he slowly said as he tied the horse's reins to a post. "She didn't."

"A shame. We were close, you know. We played together as children. I thought she would have at least mentioned me, even in a passing conversation."

"She doesn't like to talk about her life in Atlanta."

"Oh, well, there you have it." He chuckled again and patted him on the back. "She's a rather secretive devil, isn't she? You know, she didn't even tell us she was coming up here to be a mail-order bride. Her ailing father found your ad in the fireplace. I suppose she thought it burned up."

Al considered James' words. So she not only didn't want to tell him about Atlanta, but she also hadn't told anyone in Atlanta about him. Why?

Al turned to face James and forced a smile. "I should tell her that you're here." He hesitated then added, "Maybe you should stay out here. I want to make sure the house is ready."

Since James cordially agreed, Al went to the cabin and softly opened the door. His gaze went to Hazel as she was stirring the stew.

She looked over at him and smiled. "Lunch will be ready soon."

"It smells good." He glanced back at James who gave him a slight wave.

"Gilbert's taking a nap, and the stew will be good for a while on its own. Would you like to go to the bedroom and have a little fun?" she offered, her tone playful.

"Right now's not a good time." He stepped into the cabin and motioned for her to come over to him, leaving the door only open a crack so James wouldn't see them.

"What is it?" she asked as she came over to him.

"Do you know him?"

"Why? Who is he?"

He gestured for her to look outside, and she leaned toward him to get a good view of him. "He says he knows you."

She started to speak but then coughed and hurried over to the pitcher on the worktable. She coughed again and pointed to her throat. "Water," she managed to say before she coughed again and poured water into the cup. She took a big gulp of it but couldn't seem to stop coughing.

"Should I invite him in?"

She shook her head and drank more water.

"When you stop coughing, do you want to come out and see him?"

She nodded but coughed again.

"Alright. I'll let him know you'll be out to say hello." He went over the threshold and closed the door. "She'll come out here," he called out as he headed for James. "The house isn't fit for company at the moment."

"Or maybe she doesn't want to see me," James replied, a contrite smile on his face. "I'm afraid we didn't leave on pleasant terms."

That explained why she didn't rush right out to welcome her cousin, and he was sure it had something to do with the reason she never talked about her life in Atlanta. But it was still strange that she didn't sound like him. They should have sounded alike since they were from the same area.

Pushing aside the question in his mind, he turned when he heard the cabin door open. Hazel came outside, wearing a hat and covering her nose and mouth with a cloth. She was still coughing. Keeping her head low, she walked over to them.

"Oh dear, is she sick?" James asked Al.

"No, but she did come upon a coughing fit."

"Hazel, it's certainly a pleasure to see you doing so well."

She glanced up and waved at him before she coughed and lowered her head again.

Since Hazel didn't say she didn't recognize him, Al assumed that James really was her cousin. Otherwise, she would have told him this man was lying. But she didn't want to spend any time with him. That much was obvious. And that meant James was only pleasant on the surface.

"Maybe this isn't a good time," Al finally told James.

"Understandable," James said. "I came unannounced. I did send a letter, of course. Did you receive it?"

"No. Nothing came in the post office for us." That much was true. Al made it a point to check the mail every time he was in town.

"What a pity. Now I feel especially bad for catching you both by surprise. May I come by at a more convenient time?"

Al glanced at Hazel who hesitated but then nodded. "Sure. Um…tomorrow at noon?" He studied her to see if that worked for her and she offered another nod. "Yes, that will work."

"Tomorrow at noon." James tipped his hat. "I look forward to it. Nice to see you again, dear cousin."

She waved again and muttered a good-bye before launching into another coughing fit.

Al frowned as he watched James leave. He turned his gaze back to Hazel who was making a hasty retreat back to the cabin. Something was wrong.

With a sigh, he went to the cabin and opened the door in time to see her pouring stew into two bowls. She wasn't coughing anymore. That was suspicious, wasn't it?

She glanced up at him and offered what he thought was an uncertain smile. "Are you still hungry?"

"Yes," he replied, though at this point he didn't have much of an appetite, even if his stomach was telling him it was time to eat. "Hazel," he began as he shut the door and walked over to the table, "should I be wary of James?"

She picked up the bowls and took them to the table. "Oh, um...I didn't expect to see him. If I'd been able to talk, I would have welcomed him inside." She cleared her throat and let out an uneasy chuckle. "I feel so embarrassed. All that coughing, you know? It wasn't very ladylike."

He debated different things he could say but finally settled for, "Well, he'll be back tomorrow."

She hurried to grab the spoons and cups. "Yes. I'll get to talk to him then." After she sat at the table, she looked up at him. "Are you going to eat?"

With a nod, he pulled out his chair and sat across from her. He watched her as she dipped the spoon into her stew. If he was right, her hand was trembling as she lifted the spoon to her mouth. He placed his hands on his thighs and leaned forward. "Hazel, what aren't you telling me?"

She paused and slowly chewed the contents of the stew before swallowing. A long moment passed between them before she finally spoke and when she did, he knew she was lying. "Nothing. There's nothing I'm not telling you." She gestured to his bowl. "Eat up before it gets cold."

Realizing he wasn't going to get her to talk, he decided to go ahead and eat. Maybe she'd tell him later. He needed to give her a chance. And if she wouldn't, then he'd have to talk to James tomorrow to find out what was going on.

***

Sadie had to tell Al the truth. As much as she didn't want to, she knew she had to. Because if she didn't, then Hazel's cousin would. Yes, she'd gotten away with covering most of her face and pretending to cough, but that ploy would only work once. She couldn't do it again.

After she put Gilbert down for the night, she went out to the barn where Al was checking on the animals. She closed her eyes and took a deep breath. She could do this. She *had* to do this. If she didn't and James exposed her, it'd be much worse. She stood a better chance of gaining Al's sympathy if she came to him first and pleaded her case.

She opened her eyes and stepped further into the barn. Since he hadn't heard her enter, she cleared her throat to get his attention.

He turned from the horse's stall and smiled at her. "Hi there, Hazel."

She swallowed the lump in her throat. He didn't make it a habit of calling her by name, something that made it a lot easier for her to live here. Strengthening her resolve, she pressed forward. "I need to talk to you."

"Alright. Give me a moment to feed the horses?"

She nodded and watched as he put hay into the trough between the two stalls. When he was done, he set the rake aside and walked over to her.

"You want to talk in the cabin?" he asked.

"No. Gilbert's asleep and I don't want to wake him." In case Al yelled at her. She clasped her trembling hands. "I was thinking outside would be best."

"That's fine." He followed her out of the barn. "Is this about James?"

"Yes," she slowly began. "But it's probably not what you think it is." It couldn't be. There was no way he suspected she was another woman.

"I gathered that the two of you aren't friends."

"No, no we aren't. In fact," she took a deep breath, "I hadn't met him before today."

His eyebrows furrowed. "You hadn't?"

Her grip on her hands tightened. "No. I…I'm not Hazel McPherson. I'm Sadie Miller."

His tender gaze quickly changed to a guarded one so she looked away from him. She couldn't bear to make eye contact with him, knowing full well the news came as a very unpleasant surprise.

"Please hear me out before you start yelling at me," she requested.

She waited for him to respond but he didn't. And that left her with no other option but to continue. Well, she'd come this far. There was no turning back now.

"Hazel McPherson died in Omaha, Nebraska. She was on her way here but had stopped at a restaurant. That's where I found her. She was sick. She had a fever and was coughing up blood." Blinking back her tears, she forced herself to continue. "I asked for a doctor, and a couple of men helped me take her to one. The doctor said there was nothing that could save her. He said she had pneumonia. Anyway, I got a chance to talk to her and she told me to come here to marry you in her place. She couldn't marry you, you see. She died within two hours of me finding her."

After a minute of silence, he let out a sigh. "I see. And you were afraid that if you told me she died, I wouldn't want to marry you instead?"

She licked her lips. "No. I didn't tell you because I was afraid that if you knew the truth about me, you wouldn't want to marry me."

"The truth about you?"

Noting the tension in his voice, she debated the best way to tell him. Did she hint at it? Or did she come right out and say it? Either way, he was bound to be upset. "I don't know what Hazel's past was like. She didn't tell me anything about it. But she knew what I had been through. She saw firsthand how life was for me." Even now, it shamed Sadie to know that Hazel had witnessed Jefferson's treatment of her. She released her breath. "Hazel told me to marry you so that I could get a new start. She wanted things to be better for me." In a lower voice, she managed, "I was a prostitute at Madame Eleanor's Brothel." She dared a peek in his direction.

His jaw dropped and his eyes grew wide. He moved his mouth a couple of times but no sound came out until he cleared his throat. "If James hadn't shown up, were you ever going to tell me?"

Blinking back more tears, she turned her gaze away from him. "Why would I tell you something like that?"

"Because it's the truth."

"Maybe, but it's not a pleasant one."

"I had a right to know."

"And if you knew, would you have married me?"

He didn't answer her, and when she dared another look in his direction, she saw the truth on his face. He wouldn't have. Having been a gentleman who saved himself for his wife, the idea of being with a whore would have been too much for him.

Gripping her skirt so she wouldn't show him how much the realization hurt her, she said, "Then it was in my best interest to keep silent, wasn't it? Because if you hadn't married me, I would have had nowhere to go but back to the brothel in Omaha."

He winced. Well, whether he wanted to hear it or not, that was all she could do. She had no skills, no means of supporting herself, no one to go to. She had nothing. And now that she had finally come to a place she could call home with a husband and child she loved with all her heart, she didn't even know if she could keep her fairytale life. Not when she saw firsthand how much her past disgusted him.

It was on the tip of her tongue to ask him what he was going to do with her. But honestly, she didn't want to know. After a long moment, he let out a long sigh then turned back to the house, saving her from having to say or ask anything at all.

She walked to the barn and climbed the ladder to the loft and curled up in the corner. She pulled her knees up to her chest.

She tried hard not to think about what he was going to do with her now that he knew about her past. She'd rather stay with him and live in the barn than go back to that horrible brothel. Maybe she could appeal to his mercy and he'd let her stay. He might not want to touch her again. Maybe he wouldn't even want to talk to her. But maybe he'd let her stay here so she wouldn't have to go back to that life.

She didn't realize she was crying until the first teardrop fell down her cheek. After that, it was impossible to stop any of the tears. They just kept coming. She hadn't cried so hard since the night Jefferson gave her her first lesson in being a prostitute. The monster actually enjoyed her tears. But with him, it was always about control and breaking the will of every prostitute under Madame's so-called care.

She tightened her hold on her knees and prayed that Al would find it in his heart to let her stay. No matter what happened, she couldn't go back to that place. She just couldn't. Next time she saw Al, she'd tell him she'd do whatever he wanted. If she was submissive enough, maybe he'd keep her. He'd never be cruel to her. He might withhold his love, but that was the worst he'd do. He'd never be like Jefferson. Resting her forehead on her knees, she continued to cry softly into the night.

Chapter Sixteen

Al couldn't sleep. He went back to the cabin, thinking that he should sleep on everything he'd just learned. The last thing he wanted to do was act in haste. It hurt. It hurt to know she had lied to him, that she hadn't even told him she wasn't Hazel McPherson. He understood why she wouldn't have told him she'd been a prostitute. He probably wouldn't have married her had he known that. Even now, thinking of her with who knew how many men made him sick to his stomach.

He rolled onto his side and stared at the space where Hazel—no Sadie—usually slept. He didn't know what to do. Yes, he was married to her. Yes, he loved her. Even now, he couldn't help loving her. But it was too painful to go back outside and talk to her right now. All this time, he'd thought he was married to Hazel, but he hadn't been. Did that mean everything Sadie said and did was done because she thought Hazel would say and do it? Or was Sadie saying and doing it as herself?

There were so many questions he had, and he wasn't sure how to ask them. He was married to her. There was no changing that. Somehow, someway, they'd have to work through it. But could he trust her? Could he believe anything else she told him? Would she act like a different person now that he knew about her past? Or would she be the same person he thought he knew?

He rubbed his eyes, unaware that he'd been crying until he felt a teardrop on his fingers. He wished he could go back to yesterday, before James showed up. He'd been happy then. Sadie had been happy, too. They'd been happy together. But now nothing would be the same and he wasn't sure if they'd ever be happy again.

***

A hard hand pressed over Sadie's mouth. In an instant she was awake, but it took her several times of blinking before she saw the silhouette of a man hovering over her. The lamp. Why didn't she light the wick in the kerosene lamp? At first she thought she was back at the brothel with one of the men on top of her, but then remembered she had fallen asleep in Al's barn.

"Who are you?" the man growled then released his hand.

She let out a scream, but he quickly slammed his hand back over her mouth.

"If you think Allen Grover is going to come out here to save you, you're mistaken," he hissed as she fought against him. "No one cares about a whore from Nebraska."

She stilled and focused on what he was saying. It took her a moment to realize this was Hazel's cousin. What could he possibly want with her?

"Yes, I heard you tell him everything," the man said. "Is it true? Did Hazel really die? And I warn you right now, if you scream again, I'll slit your throat."

A cool blade pressed into her neck.

When he released his hand, she struggled not to scream again. It was tempting to, but she'd been around enough men to know he was serious. He would kill her or anyone else if they got in his way. She swallowed then licked her lips to moisten them. "Yes," she whispered. "Hazel died right in front of me."

"Good. Then she did inhale the poison."

Sadie didn't have time to register what he was saying because, in the next instant, he stood up and forced her to her feet.

"I've been careful," he said, sliding his arm around her waist and then going to the edge of the loft. "I can't have any loose ends."

"Wh-what are you going to do to me?" she forced out.

"I can't have you stay here." Holding her close to him, he held onto her as he descended the ladder. "You're a witness, my dear." When they reached the bottom step, he jumped off and turned her to face him, his body uncomfortably close to hers, making her sick to her stomach. "I have two options for you. I can either kill you and let that be it. Or I can take you to your brothel. I have a feeling no one listens to the silly rantings of a prostitute." He slid the knife along her cheek. "A prostitute, after all, is only good for one thing. And if you keep silent, I'll let you live, which is more than what I'll do for Allen."

She stiffened. "What did you do to him?"

"Nothing. Yet."

"No. I won't let you hurt him."

Ignoring the knife, she tried to shove him away, but his grip grew tighter. She hated this. Her lack of strength was always her undoing. No matter how much she tried to fight men, they were always stronger. They always overpowered her, doing whatever they wanted. She made an attempt to grab the knife, but he struck her on the head and everything went black.

***

The first thing Sadie became aware of was being rocked back and forth. The second thing she noted was that she was riding a horse, and a man held her around the waist. The third thing she realized was that she'd been gagged so she couldn't yell for help. Ignoring the pain in her head, she examined her surroundings.

She was traveling through the Black Hills forest. She tried to move but her wrists and ankles were tied together.

A cold blade pressed into her neck. "Here's the deal," James said. "We'll be arriving at the stagecoach soon. You're going to act like you want to be with me. I can't have anyone asking questions. You so much as give me a single problem, and I'll slit your throat. I killed that husband of yours. He isn't coming back. You have nothing to go back for."

He was wrong. She did. Gilbert. Gilbert needed her.

"And don't worry about that little brat," he added. "I took care of him, too."

She stiffened and tried to ask him if he had been such a monster that he'd kill a defenseless baby, but the cloth tied around her mouth stopped her.

"I can't have any loose ends," he muttered. "I know how attached women are to babies. I can't have you coming back here. You're lucky I'm letting you live."

Lucky? Is that what he called it? He was sending her back to a brothel and he said she was lucky? He killed her husband and child and he called her lucky? Lucky would have been if he'd killed her, too. Then at least she wouldn't have to live without them.

She blinked back her tears the best she could, but they found their way down her face anyway.

***

Al stirred from his slumber, surprised he'd managed to fall asleep at all given everything he'd just learned. He sat up in the bed. Something woke him up, but he didn't know what. Maybe Sadie had returned to the cabin. If that was the case, it meant she had been cold. He doubted she'd be coming in to see him. But even so, he wanted to see her.

He got up from the bed and glanced at the slit of light peeking through the drapes. Morning had finally come. Now would be a good time to get up and see Sadie, especially since Gilbert didn't have to be up for another hour. He wasn't sure how much he could resolve after finding out everything he did, but he was still married to her. They needed to at least agree to be cordial to each other for Gilbert's sake. He didn't expect things to get resolved right away. The wounds were too fresh. The pain too real. He just hoped she could understand that he couldn't go back to how they'd been before. He needed time to sort through everything, to get to a place where he could be at peace with it all.

After he got dressed, he opened the bedroom door, surprised when he didn't see her. He could have sworn he heard someone out here. Frowning, he went to Gilbert's room and opened his door. He didn't think Gilbert could get out of his crib, and he breathed a sigh of relief when Gilbert was fast asleep.

Closing the door, he walked across the room, thinking to go outside and look for Sadie, when he caught sight of a note on the worktable.

His gut tightened as he picked it up.

Dear Allen,

There's something else I didn't tell you but feel you should know. I poisoned Hazel so I could take her place. Now you know the truth. All of it. I can't stay here and pretend anymore.

My sincerest apologies,
Sadie

Al stared at the note for several minutes before it occurred to him what was wrong with it. She had called him 'Allen' instead of Al. She wouldn't have done that.

Which meant she didn't write the note. Someone else did. But who? Aunt Betty and Bear wouldn't. They didn't even know

Sadie's real name. There was only one person he could think of who knew what Sadie had told him last night, and that was someone who had never left his property, even though he pretended to. James. Hazel's cousin.

It made perfect sense. There was no one else it could be. He was the only logical choice.

Al bolted for the door and searched his property for any signs of Sadie or James, but he didn't find anything until he got to the edge of the barn door. There was a piece of rope on the ground. He bent down and retrieved it.

It'd been cut by someone who was in a hurry. He frowned. James? Did he bring rope with him? But why?

"Sadie?" Al called out.

The only answer he got was the singing of some birds and bleating of his two goats. That wasn't good. Something was wrong.

He continued his search, calling for Sadie, but she was nowhere to be found.

James. James took her. But why? Why write a note? The note was probably done in hopes Al wouldn't come after her, but that led him to another question: where did James take her? There was only one place he could think of, but what good would sending her back to a brothel do?

Wouldn't it have been easier if he just killed her? If she knew—or suspected—something that James didn't want to find out, then wouldn't he be better off killing her and getting rid of any potential evidence?

No, Al decided as he headed back for the cabin. If James killed her and Al found her, he'd come after James. That could get messy. It was a safer bet to write the note. Al had never seen Sadie write anything, but he knew full well if she wrote him a note, she would have addressed it to 'Al'.

He entered the cabin and quickly went to Gilbert who was still asleep. The boy was too tired to make a fuss as he quickly changed his diaper. After he was done, he grabbed his money and stuffed it into his pocket. Then he hurried out of the cabin. The ride to Bear and Aunt Betty's seemed to take forever, and with a young boy in the saddle, he didn't dare push the horse too hard.

When he got to their cabin, Bear was in the barn. He got off the horse, careful to keep Gilbert securely in his arms. "Is Aunt Betty in the house?" Al called out, sticking his head in the large doorway.

"Sure is," Bear replied and stood up from where he was milking the cow. "Something wrong?"

"Yes. But I can't go into it. I need Aunt Betty to watch Gilbert while I'm gone."

"Gone? Where will you go?"

"Omaha."

"What about Hazel?"

Al hesitated to answer but finally decided to say, "My wife and I need to go to Omaha. Something's come up that neither one of us expected."

With a nod, Bear went over to him and held his hands out. "I can tell you're in a hurry. I'll take the boy for you and tell Betty you couldn't stop to talk. And don't worry about the animals. I'll tend to them."

"Thank you." Al rubbed Gilbert's hair affectionately. "I'll be back as soon as I can."

He ran back to his horse and headed on out, hoping Sadie wasn't too far ahead of him. He might catch her before she arrived in Omaha, but he wasn't counting on it. James had a good head start. Al suspected he wouldn't see Sadie again until he was in Omaha, if that was where James was actually taking her.

***

The blue sky spanned for miles in front of Sadie, but unlike last time she was in a stagecoach, she didn't feel the sense of freedom and hope she had before. No. There was no freedom or hope where she was going. And worse, she knew what it'd been like to have someone like Al and Gilbert in her life.

Another tear slid down her cheek, but she quickly wiped her cheek on the seat of the stagecoach before James noticed she was awake. He'd made it a habit of giving her laudanum to make her sleep through her journey ever since she'd run off on the pretense of needing to visit the privy. The ploy hadn't worked. He'd been watching her behind the bushes, something she hadn't planned on. What kind of man wanted to watch a woman tend her to personal business anyway?

"Your companion is awfully quiet," a man who was riding with them told James.

She let out a soft moan and closed her eyes. Then, for good measure, she let out a light snore.

"The trip tires my cousin," James replied. "We've been on our journey now for a couple days."

"Better tired than sick," the man said with a chuckle. "Some women can't handle the constant swaying back and forth of the coach."

"My cousin's a sturdy woman. She can handle anything."

Their talk then turned to political matters, and she released her breath. Early on, she had thought to ask one of their traveling companions for help, but when James gestured to the gun under his suit jacket, she decided against it. She didn't think he planned to kill her, but he might've intended to kill the other person and she couldn't risk that.

In addition to a knife, he had a gun. He'd come prepared to kill anyone who got in his way. He had killed Hazel. She saw the effects of the poison he'd given her. Then he'd killed Al and Gilbert... Another tear went down her cheek. It was impossible to know what someone like James was capable of.

No wonder Hazel tried to run away and burned all evidence of where she was going. If only that fragment of the mail-order bride ad had burned with everything else. Poor Hazel. She had been so careful. But even the best of plans weren't guaranteed success. She did what she could. She tried. And failed. Another tear slid down Sadie's cheek. She had no idea what Hazel went through when she was taking her trip north. Was she relieved? Was she scared? Did she think she got away in time? Did she believe James hadn't discovered her plan and didn't have a way to stop her?

It was a shame Hazel hadn't told her more. But then, maybe it was just as well that she didn't know the details. Whatever Hazel had gone through, it hadn't been pleasant, and Sadie had enough unpleasantness to last her a lifetime.

Shifting so her back was to the men, she opened her eyes and looked up at the blue sky again. The color was beautiful, as always. She decided she'd always associate it with freedom and hope. She had enough of colors that were associated with dark and painful things. It was time she picked one that could always give her a sense of joy, even if that joy could never be recaptured again.

Chapter Seventeen

"Come on, dear," James said as he patted Sadie's cheek. "We're home."

Sadie could barely bring herself to open her eyes. The trip had been mostly a blur. Once she got on the train, he'd put a cloth over her mouth and nose, and whatever was on it, it kept her asleep through most of the ride in the train car. He had never left her side. Not once. Whether she ate or had to use the necessary, he was right there. And if he had to use the necessary, she was right there, too. There was no chance of escape. He left nothing to chance. Never had she encountered anyone so dangerous.

"Wake up," James said again, this time pulling her to her feet. "You need to walk."

She winced as he squeezed her arms.

"The train's about to stop," he whispered in her ear and turned her so that he was behind her. He pressed a knife into the small of her back. "Don't do anything stupid. Just walk as if everything is natural."

"You think I want to go back to Madame's?" Despite feeling groggy, she shoved at him. "You might as well kill me and get it over with."

He grabbed her by the throat and threw her to the seat. She held her head, too dizzy to regain her balance. He squeezed her arms again, his fingers digging into her flesh.

"There are things worse than death," he hissed. "No one cares about a prostitute. You think anyone will come looking for you? Don't think that husband of yours is going to. The dead can't come back for the living. Now, get up and walk or I'll show you how uncomfortable a broken bone can be."

The man wasn't bluffing. And as much as she didn't want to be at a brothel, it was better than being with him. With a heavy sigh, she struggled to stand up. But with her head still spinning, she stumbled back against the window.

He grasped her arm and shoved her at the door. "You can't honestly still be groggy from the chloroform."

She leaned against the door so she wouldn't lose her balance again. "I'm doing my best," she muttered.

"Do better than that. Now stand up straight."

She forced herself to obey and didn't fight him as he opened the door. He clasped her arm and dragged her out of the car. The train slowed but it was still difficult for her to keep up with his pace. Finally, when it came to a stop, she was able to gain some of her balance back.

The journey off the train and to the brothel was a blur. She didn't know if she wanted to be alert for any of it, so she didn't fight the sensation that told her she was in a dream. It was easier to go along with it because it dulled the pain of knowing she would never see Al or Gilbert again.

By the time they reached the brothel, she thought she was going to pass out. She was far too weak, and she wasn't sure if it was the lack of proper food and water or being constantly subdued into sleeping. Maybe it was a mixture of all those things. Or maybe it was grief. In spite of it all, she remained standing while James knocked on the door.

"Ordinarily, I would never be caught dead in a place like this," he whispered then chuckled. "A mistress is far cleaner to deal with."

"With a good doctor, even diseases can be taken care of," she snapped.

"Not all diseases."

True, but enough of them. Madame prided herself on running a clean establishment. Sadie rolled her eyes. Whether it be mistress or prostitute, she saw little difference. Both were used by men. Both received money for their services. It was nothing like being a wife who was honored and cherished. A tear slid down her cheek, and she wiped it away.

The door opened and Jefferson's gaze went to Sadie. "I didn't think I'd see you again."

"I thought I'd do you a favor and return her," James said.

"Bored of her?"

He snorted. "I didn't take her. No. She went all the way to the South Dakota Territory and took up with a man. But he doesn't want her anymore and I'm to send her back, if the price is right."

"And if Madame isn't interested?"

He shrugged. "I suppose I can drop her off at another brothel. I've seen the looks men gave her as we came here. She's a beauty. Far more beautiful than a lot of other women. I gather men would pay handsomely for a night with her."

The corner of Jefferson's mouth twitched. "Come in and I'll get Madame Eleanor."

James' hold on Sadie's arm tightened as he followed Jefferson down the hallway. Sadie brought her hand up to her mouth when they stepped into the parlor. The smell of smoke and alcohol filled the large room. The purple rug, red sofas and chairs and purple drapes only added to her nausea. She closed her eyes and thought back to the simple cabin Al owned, but all she could see was James shooting Al and Gilbert as they slept.

"You should be proud," James whispered in her ear. "These people value you enough to pay for you. I doubt they'd pay for just any whore who returned."

He pushed her toward one of the couches and sat next to her. Taking a cigar from the middle of the table in front of them, he lit it up and leaned back, crossing his legs and letting out a long puff of smoke.

Her stomach rolled and she leaned forward so her forehead rested on her knees. She concentrated on the sound of her breathing, numbering each one as she inhaled and exhaled. Again, her mind flashed back to Al and Gilbert, but the happy image was quickly replaced with a gun and James' amused snicker. The man was a monster.

"How could you do it?" she asked, finally looking up at him.

"Do what?" James asked and flicked some ashes in the nearby ashtray.

"How could you kill a baby? He was a defenseless little boy. He couldn't do anything to protect himself."

He shrugged. "Sometimes we're forced to do unpleasant things. You of all people should know that, given your profession."

"Nothing could be more unpleasant than killing a baby."

"And what good would it have done any of us if he had lived? You would have wanted to go back, and I can't have you doing that." He leaned toward her and lowered his voice. "You're the only one who can connect me to Hazel's death. I worked too long and too hard to let anyone get in my way. With her out of the way, I inherit everything."

"This is all about money?"

"You honestly can't tell me you're surprised. Men come here to seek pleasure and they give your madame money. You of all people should understand the entire world is after money."

Before she married Al, she would have agreed with him. But since she did marry him, she knew that there were people—good and honest people—who didn't use money for selfish ambition. "I feel sorry for you. You might have money, but you've lost your soul."

He narrowed his eyes at her. "You should be feeling sorry for yourself. You're the one who'll be used by men who care nothing for you."

Familiar footsteps descended the stairs. Sadie wrapped her arms around herself. She'd know Madame's ominous footsteps anywhere.

"I hear you found my wayward lady of the evening," Madame said as she entered the room.

James rose from the couch and offered a polite nod. "Indeed I have." He gestured to Sadie who refused to look at Madame Eleanor.

"Yes, she's one of mine," Madame replied. "Sadie, it's been a long time since you left us."

Sadie chose not to respond. There was nothing she could say that Madame would accept. She didn't want to think of what Madame was going to do with her once James left and she was free to put aside all pretenses of being polite.

Madame went over to a decanter and poured a glass of brandy then handed it to James. She gestured for him to sit and he did. Madame pulled up a chair and sat across from them. "I hear you wish to sell her to me."

The conversation was so eerily reminiscent of the one Sadie's mother had with her all those years ago when Sadie first came here. Sadie was so scared back then. She'd begged her mother not to do it, but her mother refused to even look at her.

"I've had her before, as you know," Madame told James. "I can't pay a virgin's price for her."

"Nor would I expect you to," he replied then sipped his brandy. "But you have to admit, she's unbelievably beautiful. I bet men pay very well for the opportunity to be with her."

Madame shifted in the chair. "Of course. We offer nothing but beautiful ladies. Do you wish to have an evening with her?"

He laughed. "I could have taken her at any time over the past week but didn't. I have a mistress who suits me better."

"Ah, but I doubt a mistress knows certain things to pleasure a man like she would. She's been trained by the best."

Sadie swallowed the bile in her throat. She didn't want to think of the lessons Jefferson gave her.

James took another puff of his cigar and smiled. "As tempting as it is, I have a train ticket set for this afternoon. I only came to sell her."

"A shame. I doubt your mistress could satisfy you like Sadie could. We have many men who return to this brothel instead of other establishments in the area for good reason."

"You certainly make a tempting offer, but as I said, I'm not going to be in Omaha for long. I only wish to sell her and be on my way."

"Very well." Madame leaned forward and made eye contact with him. "As I said, I can't offer the virgin price. Beautiful or not, a virgin is worth more when she comes to us."

"Maybe, but for all her experience, she must have some value."

"She does. All of my girls do." She took a deep breath and drummed the arm of her chair. "Twenty dollars."

"Oh come now, she's worth more than that. Her beauty alone will earn you more than that in two months."

"I see you're a shrewd businessman. Fine. Forty."

He drank the rest of his brandy and set the glass on the table. "A hundred."

"A hundred?"

"She'll earn more than that in a year. Considering you'll be using her services for longer than that, you're getting a bargain. I could ask five hundred."

Sadie didn't want to hear any more of this. It was so degrading. She didn't want to think of how much she'd earned Madame over the years she'd been there, nor did she want to go through with any of this. "This man has killed people," she blurted out. "His cousin, a man, and a baby. He has no regard for anyone but himself."

Beside her, James stiffened, but Madame laughed. "None of this concerns you, Sadie." She waved at her dismissively. "You'll have to forgive her. She will say anything to get out of doing her job."

James relaxed and smiled. "She wasn't easy to bring here."

"I can imagine. When she first came here, she made several attempts to run away and even created some rumors about the most notable customers who frequent this establishment. You're not the first one she's rambled some unbelievable stories about. It's a cry for attention, I suppose."

"Or an overactive imagination."

Sadie's face grew warm but she kept her mouth shut. All of the stories she used to tell Madame were true, but Madame refused to believe any of them. She never could figure out if it was because Madame had nothing but contempt for her or if it was because she honestly couldn't believe the men she catered to were capable of the things Sadie accused them of. But one did steal from Madame's petty cash, another did use Sadie's services more often than he paid for them, and another did poison another prostitute. What good was reporting any of it? James was right. When people looked at her, all they saw was a prostitute. And prostitutes were only good for one thing.

Madame tapped her fingers on the chair for a couple seconds then said, "Eighty dollars. That's my final offer."

James finished his cigar and seemed to think over her offer for a few seconds before he nodded. "You drive a hard bargain, but it's a deal. Eighty dollars."

With a smile, Madame rose to her feet. "I'll be right back with the money."

Sadie wondered if James was going to say anything to her since she told Madame what he did, but thankfully he didn't. Jefferson came into the room a few seconds later and went over to Sadie. It'd do her no good to fight him. He was too strong for her, and she was too tired. She followed him out of the room and up the all-too-familiar stairs she'd hoped she'd never have to climb again.

"You're in luck," Jefferson said as he led her down the hall that reeked of sex. "You can have your old room."

She placed her hand up to her nose to block out as much of the smell as possible. He stopped at the door and opened it. Avoiding eye contact with him, she entered the room. The yellow rug, the green curtains, the red bed coverings… She hated those colors, especially when they were mixed together. And now they were staring at her all over again.

Jefferson chuckled. "You know, it's ironic how you can tell Madame Eleanor the truth, but she'll never believe you."

Surprised, she looked over at him.

"I was there when that woman was dying in the doctor's office." He smirked at her. "It's not your fault, my dear. You just happened to be in the wrong place at the wrong time. And now you're back here."

Maybe she should feel better that someone believed her about James, but she didn't. With a sigh, she turned her attention away from him and sat in the little chair by the window. Back in her prison. Trapped. Just a doll to put on display to be used whenever a man wished. The familiar sense of despair swept over her.

"Really now, Sadie, it can't be too bad," Jefferson said. "If your mother had thrown you out on the street, you would have died of hunger or cold. At least this way, you have food, a roof over your head, and clothes on your back."

"And no respect."

"Respect? That should be the least of your concerns. At least that man didn't kill you."

He shut the door before she could respond. She turned her attention to the window and stared at the people as they walked up and down the street. How she envied them their freedom. The women were happy. Some of them were walking with their husbands. She caught the way a couple of the men smiled at them and remembered the way Al had smiled at her.

Her gaze went to her hand at the ring he gave her on Christmas day. She traced the rose and leaves. He had wanted it to be a reminder of their marriage, that when she looked at it, she would think of him. And she would. Every day for the rest of her life. She almost brushed away her tears, but this time she didn't. And soon, she couldn't stop crying.

Chapter Eighteen

Daylight faded into evening and Sadie hadn't moved from her spot by the window. Her tears had finally slowed to a simple trickle. Her shirtwaist was drenched but she didn't care. Her life was over. Had she not been so greatly loved, she might have been better off. But knowing what she'd lost, she didn't know if she could go on.

The door to her room opened. The familiar footsteps of Jefferson's shoes clanked across the hard floor. "Madame noticed you didn't come down for dinner," he said.

"I'm not hungry," she softly replied.

"I brought you your meal." She heard him set the tray on the table by her bed. "You must keep up your strength. Madame has given you a reprieve for tonight, but tomorrow you'll be expected to get back to work."

He left the room and shut the door behind him.

Leaning forward, she pressed her forehead against the window and closed her eyes. If only James had shot her when he shot Al and Gilbert. Then she could be with them.

She released her breath, another tear falling down her face. She imagined, just for a moment, that she was back in the cabin nestled away in the wilderness. She'd be rocking Gilbert to sleep in the chair, warm as the small fire in the cookstove continued burning. Al would come in after tending to the animals and give her a smile that spoke volumes of his love for her.

She swallowed as more tears came. It couldn't be true. Al and Gilbert couldn't be dead. But why would James lie about something like that? He had murdered Hazel. Why wouldn't he murder others?

He could have murdered her, too. He didn't have to sell her back to Madame. Maybe he wanted money, but what was eighty dollars when he stood to inherit much more than that?

Maybe he told her he killed Al and Gilbert so she wouldn't run back to Rapid City. But then what would Al think since she was gone?

She opened her eyes and sat up straight. Maybe Al would think she went back here, to the brothel. She wiped the tears from her cheeks. That was silly. He'd never believe she'd want to return here. It was a horrible existence. One that no woman should ever know.

But what if he didn't know that? He'd never been in one. He didn't know what it was like here.

She stood up, her legs stiff from the hours she'd spent sitting in the chair. She worked the kinks out as she paced the room. Maybe they weren't dead. She never saw their bodies. Never heard gunshots. She was unconscious the whole time, and when she woke up, she was on the horse.

She clasped her hands together and shook her head. No. It was impossible. They couldn't still be alive. Wouldn't she know it if they were? Wouldn't she feel something? Was someone supposed to know if someone they loved died?

She tried to remember how it was with her father when he died. He'd been working on a railway so her mother didn't know right away. But Sadie couldn't remember if her mother suspected something was wrong or not. It happened so long ago.

It was wishful thinking. That's all it was. She stopped pacing and turned to the door. But she never saw the bodies. She never heard the gunshots. If there was a chance, even a remote one, wasn't it worth it to check?

Decision made, she went to the door and opened it, checking the hallway. One of the prostitutes was taking a man to her room. Sadie quickly put her head back in her room and closed the door almost all the way so they wouldn't see her as they passed. She held her hand over her nose so she wouldn't smell the woman's perfume or the smoke and brandy on the man's breath.

When they had entered the woman's room, she slipped out of hers and tiptoed down the hallway, ignoring the glaring red carpet as much as possible. She made it to the top of the steps and listened as the men and women laughed downstairs. She could hear Madame offering the gentlemen more brandy and telling Jefferson to retrieve more cigars.

Sadie debated the best way to proceed. If everyone was distracted down there, they might not notice her. The parlor didn't lead directly to the door. The door was in the narrow hallway. But someone might see her. She glanced back down the hall where her room was. If she had something to climb down, she'd use her window. Being as it was, she didn't dare in case she broke a bone.

She'd just have to chance it. Taking a deep breath, she slowly went down the stairs, mindful to listen for anyone who might be slipping into the hallway upstairs or leaving the parlor. So far, so good. Everyone was content to stay where they were for the moment.

She picked up her pace and made it by the parlor door, but just as she reached the front door, Jefferson called out, "Going somewhere, Sadie?"

She grabbed the knob and flung the door open, but before she could even make it down the first step, Jefferson's hand wrapped around her arm. Hard.

"Nice try," he said and pulled her back inside. He shut the door and leaned against it. "You know you can't go out there. From now on, you'll never leave this place. We won't be taking our chances."

"What's going on?" Madame Eleanor asked as she hurried out of the parlor. Her eyes widened. "I should have known." Slowing her steps, she approached them, crossing her arms. "Haven't you learned anything from your little escapade?"

"You don't understand," Sadie replied, wishing Jefferson would loosen his grip. "I'm a married woman now. I have no business being here."

Madame chuckled. "You have every business being here. I paid for you. Twice, might I add. First with your mother. Then from the man who used you and got tired of you."

"He wasn't my husband." Sadie tried to pull her arm away from Jefferson, but he only tightened his grip. She winced but stopped fighting against him. "Do the decent thing and let me go back to my husband and child."

"The ones you claimed were murdered?" Madame asked.

"The man who brought me here said he killed them, but…"

"But what?"

She glanced from Madame to Jefferson, already knowing how ridiculous the whole thing seemed to them. "I never saw their bodies. I never heard the gunshots. I didn't confirm it."

At that, Jefferson's lips curled up. "Let that be a lesson to you. Make sure someone actually is a murderer before spouting off that they are."

His fingers pinching her arm, he stormed over to the stairs, dragging her along. "Please, just let me go back and see. I need to know," she pleaded.

"It's too late for that," Madame snapped. "I paid a handsome fee for you. I don't take the loss of money lightly."

"Why is it always about money for you?" Sadie demanded and fought in earnest to get away from Jefferson.

"Restrain her," Madame told him. He raised his free arm to strike Sadie, but Madame shook her head and lowered her voice. "Not her face. Men will overlook bruises everywhere but the face."

Jefferson put his arm down and shoved Sadie at the stairs. She tumbled against them.

"Is there a problem, Madame Eleanor?" a man asked.

Sadie glanced over her shoulder at the thin figure with a handlebar mustache. He left the parlor and walked over to them. She didn't remember his name. Not that she ever cared to know any of their names. It was easier if she didn't.

"Not at all," Madame replied with a smile. "The girl's had a little too much to drink and slipped. That's all."

"I remember her," he said in interest, his gaze focusing on her.

Sadie looked away and stood up. At least Jefferson wasn't holding her arm anymore. She rubbed it, wondering how long it was going to be sore.

"She was away for a while but has come back," Madame said. She went over to him and gestured to the parlor. "Care to have another brandy?"

"I've had enough, thanks." His gaze went back to Sadie. "She's lovely to look at. I would like to be with her tonight."

Sadie bristled. She never liked it when a man paid her a compliment like that, except for Al. Daring to make eye contact with him, she spat, "I'm married."

Jefferson took her arm again, and though he appeared to be gentle, the grip was tight. He led her up the stairs. She tripped another time, but he didn't slow his pace. By the time they were at her room, he threw her onto the floor and shut the door behind him.

"There will be no more of this nonsense," he seethed. "You have greatly upset Madame."

"I don't care," she yelled even as tears filled her eyes.

"You should care. Think about what you're doing. You have no money. All you have are the clothes on your back. Just how long do you think you'll live out there?"

She wiped her tears away, her face hot from a mixture of anger and humiliation. In her haste to leave this place, she hadn't given any thought to money. He was right. She would have made it to the train station and realized she couldn't get a ticket.

Jefferson muttered something under his breath but left the room, leaving her. And this time, it was dark since the sun had set. Shivering, she ran over to the small table by her bed and searched for the matches. Once she found one, she lit the wick in the kerosene lamp and searched the room for anyone who might be hiding in the shadows. It was unlikely, of course, but possible that someone had crept in here while she was gone. Not all men wanted to pay and found a way into her room without Madame or Jefferson knowing.

She relaxed after she searched the room and realized she was alone. She set the kerosene lamp on the dresser. Leaning against the dresser, she put her face in her hands. There was no way she was getting out of this. James had been very clever. Too late, she realized she made the grave error in not demanding to see if Al and Gilbert were really dead. But even if she had, he had her so heavily sedated for most of the trip that it'd been hard to think clearly. And now she was here, mentally going through every chance she'd missed at getting away from him.

His plan had worked. She was sufficiently trapped. She had no money, and there was no way Madame would let her go to one of her customers outside the brothel. No doubt tomorrow, Jefferson would be putting a lock on her door from the outside so she couldn't leave it without their permission.

Leaving right after Hazel died had been a huge risk. It'd been the most daring thing she'd ever done. And not all risks paid off. She'd known it when she took the chance and ran to the train station. She let out a long sigh and lowered her hands. This small room would be all she'd know from this moment on. Trapped. James' plan had worked perfectly. She had no way of getting to Al, and Al would believe she returned—willingly—to this place.

No wonder Hazel hadn't made it. Sadie could only guess the details of Hazel's life, but she had enough of the pieces to know she'd faced a formidable enemy. She wiped away another tear. Did the doctor ever find out who she was? Did he send word to Hazel's family in Atlanta? Or was Hazel buried in the cemetery nearby with no name or year of birth to mark her stone?

The door opened and she glanced over in time to see Madame. Madame entered and quietly shut the door behind her. Her back against the door, she looked at Sadie. "That little display down there was in bad taste, Sadie. I won't tolerate that kind of behavior again. I'd bring one of the men up here tonight to remind you of why you're here, but men don't like it when prostitutes cry. It makes them feel guilty. Thanks to your little outburst down there, the gentleman in the hallway decided to leave." She frowned at her. "And he took a lot of money with him."

Sadie turned her gaze from Madame. "I won't stop crying. I should be with my husband and child."

"It's not good to live in delusions. You need to accept the fact that you're a prostitute and you'll always be one." Sadie shook her head, but Madame clucked her tongue. "I can see this is going to be a lot of work. You've forgotten everything Jefferson painstakingly taught you."

"Painstakingly taught me?" Sadie snapped, looking back at her despite the fresh tears welling up in her eyes. "I was the one who went through the pain of everything he did."

"He's much better than others in the business. At least he told you about the cooking oil and ways to distract yourself so you didn't have to think about what you were doing. He even gives certain gentlemen sheaths to use." She pointed at Sadie and approached her. "You should be thankful for all of that. Before I had him in my employment, my ladies didn't live as long as they do now, nor were they as healthy. I run the cleanest brothel in town. Men pay good money to come here because they know that. Would you rather go to Madame Marsha's or be down at the saloon?"

"I'd rather be home," Sadie whispered.

"This is your home," Madame snapped then rolled her eyes. "It's just like having you here when you were a child. All those lessons have been lost on you. Eighty dollars was too much to pay." She groaned and gave an irritated shake of her head. "Well, it's too late for regrets. All we can do is move forward. Tomorrow Jefferson will start retraining you."

Madame's meaning took a moment to sink in and Sadie shook her head.

"You're here to please the men," Madame said, her voice firm. "While they enjoy looking at you, there's more to it than just showing them your pretty face." She motioned to the tray of untouched food. "Aren't you going to eat anything?"

"I can't," Sadie replied.

Madame's eyes narrowed at her. "You're not with child, are you?"

"No." And even if she was, Sadie would never tell the truth because then Madame would bring Jefferson in to 'resolve' that inconvenient problem.

She scanned Sadie's body. "You don't look it. When was the last time you had your cycle?"

Sadie gulped. How she hated answering these kinds of questions. "Twenty days ago," she forced out.

"Then we'll know in a few days." She picked up the tray. "You won't get anything to eat until tomorrow morning."

The last thing Sadie wanted to do was eat, even if Madame did hire one of the best cooks in Omaha.

"It's like starting over," Madame grumbled before she left the room.

Sadie placed her hand over her stomach, already sick. She couldn't be with another man. There was no way she could get through it. Not after she'd been with Al. Not after everything he'd taught her about the love that was possible between a man and a woman.

As soon as Jefferson put his hands on her, she was going to throw up. She just knew it. And then Madame would be right. It would be as if they were starting all over again because she had the hardest time being able to get through those lessons without losing her breakfast.

Closing her eyes, she crumbled to the floor and gave into the urge to cry once more.

Chapter Nineteen

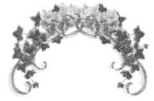

Al pushed his way off the train. Despite his exhaustion, he had to keep going. He wasn't going to stop until he got Sadie back. It wasn't going to be easy. He might not know anything about brothels, but he doubted the owner would be willing to just hand Sadie over to him.

"Excuse me," he told an old man when he bumped into him on the way down the steps off the train.

Once his feet hit the platform, he ran over to one of the baggage handlers.

"Sir, may I please interrupt?" he asked as someone took the brass tag from the baggage handler.

The baggage handler and the man turned to him.

"I'm in a hurry," Al explained. "All I need to know is where something is."

The man nodded and tipped his hat. "Go ahead. I'm done."

As he left, Al looked back at the baggage handler. "Do you know where I can find Madame Eleanor's Brothel?"

The baggage handler rolled his eyes. "You don't have an emergency."

The baggage handler turned away from him, but Al grabbed his arm. "Yes, I do. My wife was abducted and taken there. I need to get her."

The baggage handler shook his arm away and straightened his uniform. "If you're going to lie, the least you could do is come up with a believable story."

"It is the truth. It happened..." Al stopped himself. The man didn't need to know the details. "Fine. Whether you believe me or not, can you tell me where to go or should I report you to your superior for not taking care of a patron?" Al held up his ticket stub to show him he'd been on the train.

The man stiffened. "There's no need for that. You can find the brothel six blocks from here." He pointed to the left. "Go that way three blocks, take a right, go two more blocks, and take a left. It's on the right."

Al hesitated for a moment, wondering if this uppity young man had been there. He sure seemed to know how to find it easily enough. Maybe he'd been with Sadie. Shaking off the image, he mumbled a thanks—only because society dictated he show his manners—and hurried down the platform.

Keeping in mind the man's directions, Al ran down the boardwalk, lanterns lighting his way as he went. He glanced over his shoulder and saw a man on a horse galloping down the street. Irritated, he stopped and waited for the man to ride by before crossing it. There weren't nearly this many people in Rapid City, and it annoyed him to no end that he had to either dodge or wait for so many. The longer it took him to get to the brothel, the greater the chance that he'd find someone in bed with his wife. And if that happened...

He shook off the mental image from his mind. No. He wouldn't use his gun to hurt anyone. He'd only use it to get her out of there. That was it. It was a threat. Nothing more.

By the time he reached the brothel, the adrenaline pumping through his body prompted him to bang on the door. Above the door was a sign that read *Madame Eleanor's Establishment*. He grimaced. Why didn't these people just call this place what it was? Why pretty it up as if it was something respectable?

He banged on the door again, and this time it opened right away. An older man in a well-dressed suit stood in front of him. Before waiting for him to speak, Al said, "I came for Sadie Gro...Miller."

The man snorted in amusement. "What man doesn't come for the prettiest one we got?" He clasped his hands in front of him. "I'm afraid she's not available tonight. You'll have to wait about a week. In the meantime, we have other ladies—"

"I'm not here as a customer," Al snapped and shoved him aside so he could enter the place. She was here. That was all he needed to know. "I'm her husband. Where is she?"

"Jefferson, what's all the commotion about?" a woman wearing a modest dress asked as she came into the entryway.

"I'm Sadie Miller's husband," Al told her. "Where's my wife?"

"A mad man," Jefferson replied with a shrug. "Seems like it's one of those days around here."

"I didn't come here to talk," Al spat then walked to the parlor.

He stopped in the doorway. Yes, he knew in theory what happened here, but it wasn't anything like he imagined. He had thought the prostitutes would be scantily clad, sitting on men's laps, flirting with them. But it wasn't the scene he witnessed. The women were wearing very little. That much was right. But none of them looked happy to be there. Not truly happy. A couple giggled, but it was forced. One was staring at something in the corner of the room. Another closed her eyes and winced. Music drifted from the phonograph, playing loud enough to hinder any real conversations that they might have engaged in. The men fondled the women between sips of brandy, oblivious to the fact that the women didn't want them there.

His mind flashed back to the first nights he'd been with Sadie. The women looked just like she had. They were forcing themselves to be with the men. But they really wanted to be somewhere else. Why didn't the men notice it? Maybe they did but they didn't care because they were only interested in satisfying their needs.

He swallowed. No wonder Sadie hadn't understood why he wanted to wait until the time was right. And now he knew why it was so important they didn't rush that part of their marriage. Sadie had been miserable here. She ran to be with him because she needed to get out of this place.

He recalled the night she'd told him the truth.

"If James hadn't shown up, were you ever going to tell me?" he'd asked her.

She'd turned her gaze away from him. "Why would I tell you something like that?"

"Because it's the truth."

"Maybe," she'd softly said, "but it's not a pleasant one."

"I had a right to know."

"And if you knew, would you have married me?"

He didn't answer her question because he knew she wouldn't have liked what he'd say. He had wanted to say yes, but he couldn't. The truth was, he would have asked her to return to the stagecoach, and he even would have paid for her fare back to Omaha. She did the right thing in not telling him. In lying, she had saved herself from this life. Not that it was much of a life. All these women, who looked as if they'd given up all hope, were waiting to die so their misery could end.

Forcing his eyes off the couples who had stopped what they were doing so they could stare at him, he reminded himself that he was going to get Sadie out of there. He'd get her out and she'd never have to be at a place like this ever again.

He turned from the parlor and came nose to nose with Jefferson. "You have no business being here," Jefferson growled then pushed him further into the hallway. "Sadie belongs here. Madame paid for her."

Before he had time to think, Al struck Jefferson across the jaw, sending him stumbling until his back hit the wall. He fell to the floor in an unconscious heap.

"There's no need to get violent," Madame Eleanor said, her tone indignant as she stared at him with wide eyes. "I run a peaceful establishment."

Ignoring her, Al ran for the stairs.

Al made it to the top and his gaze swept the hallway. He cursed under his breath. All the doors were closed.

"Sadie!" he yelled, hoping she'd come out of her room.

God knew he didn't want to open the wrong door and find a man intimately engaged with a prostitute. But what if that prostitute was Sadie? His jaw clenched. He'd get the man off of her faster than he could blink, that's what he'd do.

A door opened and he headed for it, hoping it was her. "Sadie?" he called out as he came closer.

Sadie peered into the hallway. "Al?" she asked, sounding as if she wasn't sure it was really him.

Al hurried in her direction, relieved to see she was fully clothed. He finally reached her and brought her into his arms, holding her tightly to him. "I'm sorry." He cupped her face in his hands and kissed her lips, her cheeks, her neck. "I'm so sorry, Sadie. Please forgive me." He brought his arms back around her and buried his face in the nape of her neck, inhaling the wonderfully comforting scent of her soap. "I had no idea how bad it was for you before we got married."

"Y-you came for me?" she whispered, still not sounding sure.

He lifted his head so he could look into her eyes.

She blinked a few times. "Am I dreaming?"

Despite the circumstances, he chuckled. "No. No, you're not, sweetheart. I'm here. And I never should have left you that night you told me the truth. I should have taken you with me into the house."

"He took me." She cleared her throat. "Hazel's cousin. James. He told me you and Gilbert were dead."

"No, we're alive. Gilbert's with Aunt Betty and Bear."

He almost told her about the letter James had left but figured they could talk about everything later. Right now he had to get her out of here. Wrapping his arm around her shoulders, he turned toward the door in time to see Jefferson standing in the doorway, his nose bloody.

Sadie gasped and clung to Al.

"Get out of our way," Al demanded, not willing to let go of his wife. Now that he found her, he wasn't going to release her. "We're going home, and you're not stopping us."

"That's not for you to decide. It's Madame's choice what happens to her property," Jefferson replied in a tightly controlled voice.

"Sadie's not anyone's property," Al barked and pulled out his gun.

"Al?" Sadie whispered.

He squeezed her shoulders. "Get out of our way," he told Jefferson.

Jefferson's eyes went to the gun. "There is the matter of payment. If you are so insistent on having her, you'll have to buy her."

"I'll do nothing of the sort. Now, go!" Al waved his gun, gesturing for Jefferson to let them pass.

Anxious footsteps came down the hallway, and Jefferson moved aside in time for Madame Eleanor to see what was going on. "He's demanding I let them go, Madame," Jefferson told her. "But I insisted he pay first. Needless to say, he's not willing."

"No, I'm not," Al said. "And if you don't let us go, I'm going to start shooting the ceiling and telling everyone in this place that you're holding a husband and wife here against their will."

Madame gasped. "You wouldn't!"

Al cocked his gun and pointed it at the ceiling.

"Let him go," Madame finally said. "The men are already getting skittish with all the commotion. I can't afford to lose all this business. A couple of the men downstairs already left. As soon as the ones up here are done, who knows if they'll even come back?"

Jefferson sighed. "Very well. Go. But be quiet on your way out. We don't want to upset anyone else."

Relieved, Al strengthened his hold on Sadie and led her out of the room. They moved aside for them, and though Sadie glanced over her shoulder, Al refused to give them the satisfaction of looking back. He didn't make eye contact with any of the men or women who watched him and Sadie as they walked out of the brothel. It wasn't until they were on the street that he felt safe enough to put his gun away.

He felt the tension ease from his body as he led Sadie down the street. She was back with him, where she belonged. That was the important thing. He pulled her closer to him, glad she continued to hold onto him. It assured him she was with him. More importantly than that, she wanted to be with him. And after seeing where she'd been, getting an idea of what she'd been forced to do… He held her more tightly to him.

His steps slowed and he glanced around them, making sure no one was following them from the brothel. Assured when he saw they were alone, he kissed her temple. "Sadie, I'm sorry I didn't take more time to listen to you."

"You were upset, and you had every right to be. I lied to you about who I was."

"Yes, but I should have heard you out instead of running to the cabin."

"Al, wait." She stopped walking so he turned to her. "It wasn't easy lying to you. I was just afraid."

He cupped her face in his hands and caressed her cheeks, noting that her eyes were still puffy from all the crying she'd done earlier that day. He didn't need further proof to know how much it pained her to be at the brothel. "What you must have gone through at that place," he whispered. "No one can blame you for being scared of what would happen to you. You didn't have anyone else to help you. I was the only person you could go to in order to get out of that life."

She nodded. "I found Hazel by chance in a restaurant. She was coughing up blood, so I took her to the doctor." She swallowed. "She didn't make it. Before she died, she told me she was on her way to marry you. She gave me her purse and the letter you sent her. She knew what I'd been going through and wished to rescue me. You would have liked her, Al. She was a very nice person."

"I have no doubt she was. What happened to her was tragic. There's no denying that. But Sadie, I hope you understand that you're nice, too. I've had a lot of time to think about our marriage on my way to find you, and there was no way you could have pretended to be someone else that entire time. You might have been using Hazel's name, but you were Sadie the whole time. You were worth rescuing." Tears filled her eyes and he gently brushed them away when they slid down her cheeks. "It's not important that you used to be a prostitute. What's important is that you're my wife. And I'm the luckiest man in the world because I have you in my life."

"Thank you, Al," she replied, her voice breaking on his name.

He gave her a soft kiss. "Let's find a place to sleep for the night. Then we can talk more in the morning, alright?"

"Alright."

His arm wrapped around her shoulders, he guided her down the next street.

Chapter Twenty

Sadie stirred from her sleep, afraid it'd all been a dream and that she was still at the brothel. But when she opened her eyes, she saw Al watching her in the dim light of the kerosene lamp, his hand tracing her breasts. He smiled at her and brought her into his arms. The sheets were still tangled from their recent round of lovemaking, but judging by his erection, he was ready to go again.

Sliding her hand between them, she stroked his penis and gave him a playful grin. "I thought you wore yourself out earlier."

"Wore myself out? I was just getting started." He rolled her onto her back and kissed her.

Closing her eyes as he deepened the kiss, she gave into the comfort and joy of being intimate with him. This was how it should be when a woman made love to a man. It should be something she looked forward to, something she could enjoy.

His tongue brushed hers, and a low moan escaped her throat. She wiggled against him, her sensitive nub pressing against his arousal. A spark of pleasure coursed through her. She began to rock her hips, encouraged when the pleasure grew stronger.

His tongue sparred with hers, making her aware of his increasing desire for her. She focused on the way he smelled, the way he tasted, the way he groaned. All of it was wonderful because it was all coming from him. Her body responded so easily to him. Already, she detected the heated wetness between her legs, prompting her to grow more insistent as she continued rubbing intimately against him. And soon he was moving his hips in time with hers. She gave herself completely to the moment and soon, her body exploded with pleasure.

His mouth left hers and he kissed her neck, murmuring her name. When she relaxed, she wrapped her legs around his waist and took him into the warmth of her body. He let out a low moan and proceeded to make love her.

In the dim light, she examined his face, noting the way he looked as he made love to her. She wanted to sear the image into her memory forever so she would never remember any of the other men who'd done this to her. They hadn't ever made love to her. All they'd done was satisfy themselves by using her. But Al was expressing his love for her, and that made all the difference.

At one point, he opened his eyes and for a moment, his thrusting slowed. "Sadie," he whispered.

She swallowed and nodded. She had no idea that it'd make her feel so vulnerable for him to call her by name during this act.

"I love you, Sadie."

"I love you too, Al," she replied, blinking back her tears. He really did love her. And it seemed much more profound that he should say it while making love to her.

He lowered his head and kissed her before he resumed his lovemaking. Her hips rose to take him in deeper. They worked together, both striving for the same goal, each one needing to be claimed by the other. She was his and he was hers. That was the way it had been since they married and it would be that way for the rest of their lives.

She tightened her hold on him and murmured his name. Deep in her core, she became aware of the now-familiar mounting pleasure that would result in her release. Deciding to pursue it, she rolled him onto his back and rocked her hips, sliding her sensitive nub intimately against him, an action which intensified her pleasure.

"Yes, Sadie. Come for me, honey."

Letting out a cry, she did, her body growing still as her flesh clenched around him. Once the waves subsided, she began rocking her hips again, this time with the intention of satisfying him. He thrust deeper into her, going with the rhythm she had established. And soon, he grew taut and she stopped moving. He throbbed inside her as he released his seed.

Once he relaxed, she settled in his arms. Not in any hurry to get off of him, she remained where she was. She didn't think she'd ever enjoy the feel a man's penis inside her, but she did with Al. And being so intimately connected to him even after lovemaking was a very pleasant experience. It took a couple minutes before her breathing returned to normal. He wrapped his arms protectively around her, and she smiled.

"I think I might be able to go back to sleep now," he whispered.

"You're finally satisfied?" she teased, lifting her head so she could look at him.

"At the moment," he replied and kissed her. "But don't be surprised if I wake you up again."

"I'd be disappointed if you didn't." Her smile widening, she rested her head on his shoulder and soon fell back to sleep.

***

The next morning, Al took Sadie to the doctor she'd been to that fateful afternoon when she found Hazel in the restaurant. Just walking into the small room and seeing the bed brought back all the memories she'd relived many times over the past few months.

"May I help you?" the doctor asked as he stood up from his desk and approached them.

Al shut the door and went over to Sadie's side, his strength a much needed comfort to her. He placed his hand on the small of her back but looked at the doctor. "Last September, my wife came here with a sick woman. Her name was Hazel McPherson. She was coughing up blood and had a fever."

"She had reddish brown hair and was wearing a dark blue dress," Sadie added. "You said she had pneumonia." She cleared her throat. "She died a couple hours after she got here."

"I remember her," the doctor softly replied. "And I remember you."

"Did you ever find her next of kin?" she asked.

"No, I didn't. There was nothing to identify where she came from."

"She was on her way to marry me," Al spoke up. "I had posted a mail-order bride ad and she answered it. I never got a chance to tell her father what happened to her."

"She's in the cemetery a few blocks from here," the doctor replied. "I'm sorry but I can't tell you anything else."

"What you told us is fine," Al assured him. "I know where to send the letter. I just wanted to be sure I could tell him where her body is."

The doctor nodded. "It's never easy to lose someone that young. You said you married Sadie?"

The doctor turned his gaze to Sadie who quickly looked away. The doctor knew she used to work at Madame Eleanor's, and though Al did as well, she really hoped he wouldn't bring it up.

"Yes, I married her," Al replied, his hand still on her back. "Best thing that ever happened to me."

"I'm glad," the doctor said. "For both of you."

Sadie glanced at him and caught the doctor's smile. Relaxing, she returned the smile. "Thank you."

Al tipped his hat and led Sadie out of the building.

"You know how to contact her father?" Sadie asked.

"I do but the address is back at our home. I can't send a letter until we're back in Rapid City." As they headed down the street, he added, "Let's find out when the next train leaves. If there's still time to eat, we'll catch breakfast at a restaurant. If not, we'll eat on the train."

"I'll be happy if I never see Omaha again."

He cupped her elbow with his hand. "You won't have to come back here. I promise you that."

She looked up at him, picking up on the tenderness in his eyes. "I love you, Al."

He gently squeezed her elbow. "I love you too, Sadie."

In silence, they walked to the train station.

***

A day after Al and Sadie returned to Rapid City, Sadie was hanging up the laundry behind the cabin when she heard Aunt Betty's familiar greeting. She paused, the clothespin hovering over Gilbert's blanket. But then she quickly secured the blanket to the line and picked Gilbert up from where he was playing in the grass. She took a deep breath to steady her nerves and went to the front of the cabin where Aunt Betty was standing by the door, a basket in her arms.

After a moment, Sadie pressed forward. "Hi, Aunt Betty."

The older woman turned in her direction. "I missed you when Al came by to get Gilbert yesterday."

She shifted so that the boy was better settled on her hip. "I thought it might be best if I didn't stop by." She cleared her throat. "In case you didn't want me there."

Aunt Betty put the basket down and headed over to her. "Oh Sadie, of course I wanted to see you. Al told us what happened, and it just broke our hearts to think of everything you've been through. No one can blame you for doing what you did, and the way I understand it, Hazel wanted you to get a new start on life."

Sadie blinked back her tears and nodded. "She did. I have a lot to be thankful for because of her."

The woman brought Sadie into her arms and gave her a warm hug that let Sadie know everything was going to be alright. She really wasn't going to hold anything Sadie had done against her.

"Thank you, Aunt Betty," she whispered.

The woman laughed as she released her. "Al's like my nephew and you're like my niece. You're family. And in this family, we all take care of each other." She cupped Sadie's face in her hands and brushed her tears away. "Now, I won't have any more crying. I came to bring you some things I thought you could use."

"You didn't have to do that."

"I know, but I wanted to." She turned to Gilbert and tapped his nose, an action which made him laugh. "I got something for you, too, mister. Come on."

She gestured for Sadie to follow her, and Sadie did. Sadie opened the door and set Gilbert on the chair, but as she suspected, he crawled over to Aunt Betty who sat on the couch.

"I thought you'd be tired of me by now," Aunt Betty said. When he reached for the basket, she chuckled. "How silly of me. It isn't me he's interested in. It's the basket of goodies."

"You're much too kind, Aunt Betty." Sadie sat next to her. "You're going to spoil us."

"I'm not doing anything I wouldn't do for anyone else in my family. And besides, it keeps me busy. I can't stand to sit around when I could be doing something. An active mind is a healthy mind."

"I can't argue that one."

She lifted the lid from the blanket and glanced around the cabin. "Is Al in the barn?"

"No. He went to town. He's sending Hazel's father a letter explaining what happened to her."

Aunt Betty patted Gilbert's back as the boy held onto her leg to maintain his balance. "Al said Hazel probably died because her cousin poisoned her."

Sadie nodded. "James said she inhaled the poison. Whether or not that's true, I don't know, but I was there when she died, and she was in a lot of pain. It was horrible."

"I bet it was."

"I hate for her father to get the letter because it's bound to devastate him, but he needs to know."

Aunt Betty clasped her hand. "Yes, he does. Even though it's painful, he should know what happened to her. You and Al are doing the right thing."

Sadie placed her hand over Aunt Betty's and squeezed it. "Thank you."

She released Sadie's hand and turned her attention back to the basket. "I got Al something, but it's nothing he needs to eat right now."

"You made him something to eat?"

"Just some candy. Licorice mixed with toffee."

"Sounds like an interesting combination."

Aunt Betty laughed and took out a bowl with candy in it. "It's a favorite in my house. I had to fend my husband away from this bowl so he wouldn't eat all of it."

Sadie giggled at the image of Bear trying to sneak all the candy for himself.

"You ought to try one. It is a good treat," Aunt Betty said as she handed it to Sadie.

She accepted a piece of the tough candy and bit into it.

"You might want to let it melt in your mouth a bit before chewing," Aunt Betty said.

Sadie decided to do just that and watched as Aunt Betty dug through the basket.

"Now," the older woman began, "I know these are old blocks, but Gilbert played with them the whole time he was at my home. I hope you don't mind if I give them to him."

"That's very thoughtful of you," Sadie replied despite the sweet candy in her mouth.

"It's nothing. One of my boys makes them."

"Your family seems to know how to do everything."

Aunt Betty grinned as she took ten wooden blocks out of the basket and showed them to Gilbert. Gilbert let out an excited cry and grabbed them. Some of the blocks tumbled onto the floor. He quickly sat down to gather them.

"It helps to be able to take care of yourself when you live all the way out here," Aunt Betty said.

"I can see that." Sadie took a good look at the blocks and shook her head. "Let me guess. The teeth marks were from Gilbert?"

"You can't blame a baby for teething. It's something they all do."

"And he puts everything in his mouth."

"That's normal. So, how does the candy taste?"

"It's good." Sadie was finally able to chew it with ease. "I can see why Al likes it. I'll put it on the table before Gilbert gets into it."

As she went over to the worktable to set the bowl down, Aunt Betty pulled out a bonnet. "This is for you."

Sadie returned to her and sat down again. "It's lovely."

"It'll keep you cooler in the summer. A hat is fine, of course, but a bonnet is better when the air is warmer. Your hair won't be so sweaty. I don't know about you, but I hate it when my hair is pressed down with sweat on my head because of a hat."

"It isn't the most comfortable feeling in the world."

"Exactly. That's why we have bonnets." She handed it to Sadie then picked out curtains. "I hope you don't mind. I made these while you were gone. It helped me believe that I would see you again."

Sadie took the curtains and unfolded them, exposing the pretty color. "They're blue. Like the sky."

"I remember you said you loved blue because you kept watching the sky when you came up here to marry Al. While I was sewing them, I imagined you and Al were coming back on the stagecoach, and I kept thinking that you were looking at the sky."

"That's lovely, Aunt Betty. Now when I look at them, I will think of coming up here with Al."

"Good."

Sadie clasped the woman's hand and smiled at her. She was very fortunate to have such a good friend. "Thank you. For everything."

"Anytime, Sadie." She squeezed her hand. "Anytime."

Chapter Twenty-One

By late August, Sadie knew she had conceived. She held off on saying anything until she passed the first couple months of her pregnancy. Her other pregnancies hadn't lasted beyond the second or third month because Jefferson took measures to make sure she'd miscarry. But she wouldn't be forced to miscarry this one. Al wanted this child. He'd be happy with the news, what with all his talk about giving Gilbert a brother or sister.

She smiled from where she stood by the sink as she glanced over at Gilbert who was walking around the main room in the cabin with a pan and spoon. Despite the noise he made as he banged them, she had to admit it was cute that he could so easily entertain himself.

She finished washing the dishes from their late breakfast and set the last plate on the towel to dry. Even with the window open, the little cabin was hot. She wiped her forehead then went over to the door and opened it. "Come on, Gilbert. Let's go outside."

He headed over to her, still holding the pan and spoon.

Chuckling, she gestured for him to put them down. "Leave those here. You can play with them when you come back in."

Though she meant for him to put the things down on the chair or table, he dropped them right on the floor and ran to the door. She laughed and caught him before he got to the porch. "You're certainly quick, aren't you?" She kissed his cheek and he rewarded her with a laugh. "You can't get too far from me. I need to make sure you're safe."

"Mama," he said and wrapped his arms around her neck.

This time her face warmed from pleasure instead of the early afternoon heat. "Yes, I'm your mama. And you're my little boy. There's nothing that will change that."

She kissed his cheek and thought to carry him down the porch steps, but he wiggled out of her arms. With a sigh, she set him on his feet, thinking of the times he used to be content to let her hold him. Now it seemed all he wanted to do was run off to explore the world around him. She gathered her skirt in one hand and held his other hand to help him down the steps. Then she released his hand and walked with him, letting him take his time touching blades of grass, a couple of leaves, a few rocks, and even a grasshopper that quickly jumped away from him.

After about fifteen minutes, Gilbert stopped to look up and called out, "Papa."

She turned her gaze in the direction he was heading and saw that Al had returned from town. He waved at them and slowed the horses until they came to a stop. "You two out enjoying the day?" he asked.

"Yep," she replied. "I see you got quite a few things." She gestured to the back of the wagon that had some crates full of staple items in them.

"I did. I also got a letter from Hazel's father."

She hesitated but asked, "What did he say?"

"I don't know yet. I didn't want to open the letter until I got home. Thought I'd read it to you."

"Alright. I think it's time for Gilbert's nap. I'll take care of him, and then we'll see what the letter says."

"I'll bring in the crates while you're doing that."

Sadie picked Gilbert up and took him into the house. She took a deep breath and went through the process of changing his diaper then settled him into the crib. Al had sent Hazel's father a letter as soon as they got back from Omaha, but even so, she hadn't expected an answer this quickly.

But it was here now and as anxious as she was to hear what Hazel's father had to say, she was also dreading it. What if James got away with it? What if her father would never believe what Al wrote? What if her father thought she killed Hazel in order to marry Al and had lied about the whole thing?

Wiping her sweaty palms on her skirt, she went to the window and pushed the blue curtains aside so the breeze could come into the room. She'd put blue curtains in every room. She wasn't going to do it at first, but after seeing them in the main room, she quickly decided she wanted every room in the little cabin to have them. And now, as she looked at the curtains, she was reminded of her journey up here with Al.

Al had seen firsthand what Sadie's life had been like at the brothel. He'd talked to the doctor. He knew she was telling him the truth about the day she met Hazel. That was what mattered.

Reassured, she left the room. She caught sight of the pan and spoon on the floor and picked them up. While she set them on the table, Al came into the cabin with a crate and put it on the worktable next to the other three crates.

"That's the last one," he said then wiped his hands on his bandana. "Is Gilbert sleeping?"

"His eyes were getting heavy when I left his room. He'll be asleep soon. Did you want to go outside?"

"It'd be cooler out there."

She accepted his hand, and they walked out of the cabin. He shut the door and motioned to the rocking chairs he'd put there earlier that summer. She was ready to sit in the one next to him, but he wrapped his hands around her waist and pulled her onto his lap.

Giggling, she shifted so that she was comfortable and kissed him. "Did you miss me?"

"I did. I'll have to see if Aunt Betty will watch Gilbert while we go into town again. I like going there with you and having you all to myself."

"I like it, too." She brushed his cheek with her fingers, noting the hint of stubble on it. She lowered her head and kissed him, this time letting her lips linger on his for a few seconds. When she lifted her head, she caught a mischievous spark in his eye. "What's going through that mind of yours?"

"I was just recalling what we did the first time we were on our way to town."

Her eyes grew wide as she fought back the urge to smile. "What did we do?"

"You know…you pulled my pants down and had your way with me."

"Had my way with you? You were the one removing my shirtwaist and chemise."

"You invited me to do it."

"I did?"

"Yes. I don't recall your exact words, but you said something along the lines of, 'Make love to me.'"

"Hmm…" She shook her head. "I don't recall saying such nonsense."

"Nonsense?"

Catching his bewildered expression, she giggled and kissed him. "I was just teasing. Of course I remember it. I remember everything about that day. The way the trees looked, the way the air smelled, how blue the sky was, and how cool the air felt on my back."

"We made love for the first time and all you can remember is the forest?"

"I remember other things, too," she assured him and kissed his cheek. "I remember how warm your hands were on my breasts, how you brought me to completion, and how good you felt as you moved inside me."

"Now that's better," he replied and kissed her. "I'd hate to think you got more enjoyment out of being in the woods than making love to me."

"I enjoy the woods as much as I do because we made love there. Just as I enjoy our bedroom and the worktable and a couple other places where we've been intimately engaged."

"We haven't done it in the loft of the barn."

"I'd like to." Especially since she'd never done it there with anyone else. It'd be another new experience, and she loved those most because they connected her to him—and only him.

"Before we venture over there, I want to read the letter." Securing his arm around her waist, he shifted so he could pull out the folded up envelope in his back pocket.

"Alright," she began as he settled back into the chair, "but before you read it, I have something important to tell you."

"What is it?"

"Gilbert will be getting a baby brother or sister at the end of February."

A grin spread across his face. "He will?"

"Yep," she replied, returning his smile. "Are you happy?"

"Of course I'm happy. We get another child and Gilbert gets someone to play with. It's wonderful news." He kissed her and gave her waist a gentle squeeze. "And just think, we already know how to change diapers and everything else."

"Gilbert's done a good job of preparing us."

"He sure has."

That news aside, she took a deep breath and pointed to the envelope. "I guess you should read it."

With a nod, he pulled the letter out of the envelope. "You know, I ought to teach you how to read this winter when there's not much else going on. Then you can finally read those dime novels to get a break from me and the children when we get on your nerves."

"Oh stop." She playfully nudged him. "I love being in this cozy little cabin with all of you."

"Just wait until after the baby is born and it's constant chaos."

She shook her head as he opened the letter. She just couldn't believe she'd ever want a break from him and their children, no matter how sure he seemed of it.

Al turned his attention to the letter and started reading it. "'I feared the worst when I never received a letter from Hazel. I was aware she wasn't happy but didn't know the details. It's unfortunate she didn't feel safe enough to come to me and tell me her misgivings about her cousin James. No one would have suspected he was capable of hurting anyone, but after confronting him, he confessed to poisoning her and then abducting your wife. He said he did it for the inheritance. His father, who is my brother, lost all his money after the war. I suppose the thought of losing everything was too much for James to handle. Shortly after his confession, he hung himself. I don't know whether to be relieved or not that the truth has come to light. I loved Hazel. She was my only child. I had loved James, too. He was my brother's only son. I used to think money would make me happy. But right now, I'd give up everything just to have Hazel back. Thank you for telling me what happened. I wish you and Sadie the best.'"

Al set the letter down and sighed.

Sadie swallowed the lump in her throat. "I suppose there was no way the letter could have had good news in it."

"No, I guess not." Al rested his head on her shoulder and tightened his hold on her. "I love you, Sadie. Nothing's going to change that. But I sure wish things hadn't turned out the way they did for Hazel and her family."

Sadie closed her eyes and kissed the top of his head. "I wish things had turned out better for them, too." She didn't feel sorry for James. But her heart ached for Hazel who'd done all she could to escape and for her father and uncle who'd never get their children back. "Life can be full of pain."

"Parts of it will be painful. That's why you have to make the most out of the good times."

He was right. And she vowed she would because that was what Hazel had wanted for her when she told Sadie to take her place as Al's mail-order bride. She had wanted Sadie to be happy. She released her breath. She would always remember Hazel, and she would always be grateful to her for the life she'd given her.

***

On the first of March, Sadie held her newborn daughter in the rocking chair by the window as the sun set for the day. She couldn't help but marvel at how perfectly formed she was. Ten little fingers and ten little toes. She had Al's nose and chin and her hair color. A perfect mix of her parents.

She was only three days old, but Sadie still couldn't get over the fact that she was really there. Though Aunt Betty had warned her to get as much sleep as possible, she'd gotten very little rest since her daughter's birth. Tonight, she'd be good and go to bed as soon as the little girl fell asleep.

But for now, the little girl was still awake, her eyes wide as she examined everything in the room. Gilbert, who'd been playing with the wooden horse and rider she and Al gave him over a year ago, came over to her. He was almost two years old now, and he looked so much like a little boy instead of a baby.

She smiled at him and rubbed his shoulder. "Did you want to see your sister?"

Gilbert peered over at the girl. "Sitter."

Sadie chuckled. "Close enough." She leaned forward and kissed his forehead. "When she gets older, the two of you will have a lot of fun together. You two can play with blocks, learn how to ride a horse, help your pa with the animals, go for walks, and lots of other wonderful things. There's a whole world out there to explore. Lots of good moments ahead to enjoy." She glanced between him and the girl. "You two are going to have a wonderful childhood. Your pa and I will see to that. I promise."

The door opened and Al smiled at them as he stepped into the house. "The animals are good for the night." He set his hat and coat on the hooks by the door and approached them. "Have you decided on a name for her yet?"

"I think so," Sadie said. "I'd like to name her Hazel. I think it'd be a good way to honor Hazel's memory."

Al knelt beside her and rubbed her back. "I think that's a great idea. We have a lot to be thankful to her for."

She nodded. "It's good that her father's new wife is expecting. He'll have another child this fall."

"The new child won't replace Hazel, but he doesn't have to be alone anymore."

"I feel better knowing that."

"I do, too," Al said. "I'll take care of our daughter tonight so you can get a good night's sleep. You don't do anyone any good when you're so tired you can't remember the difference between flour and baking powder."

"It was an easy mistake," she replied. "Anyone could have made it."

"Maybe, but it doesn't make for good pancakes."

She laughed. "At least we had some leftover muffins from Aunt Betty."

Grinning, he brought Gilbert into his arms. "You think you might want to go out to the barn with me tomorrow and help out?"

"Yes," Gilbert replied, giggling as Al tickled him.

Al looked over at her. "Next week we'll pay Aunt Betty and Bear a visit. I'm anxious to give them the skin from that elk I caught."

"I'm looking forward to it," Sadie said. "It was nice of her to help me when I was giving birth to Hazel."

"I think she would have been disappointed if she couldn't be here. She loves to help out whenever she can. She says it makes her feel useful." Al got to his feet and picked Gilbert up. Leaning forward, he kissed her. "After I put him in bed, I'll take care of Hazel so you can go to sleep."

"Thank you, Al. And good night, Gilbert."

"Bye, Ma," Gilbert replied.

To her surprise, Al bent down and gave her another kiss. "I love you, Sadie."

Her smile grew wider. "I love you too, Al."

She watched him as he took Gilbert to the bedroom before she turned her gaze back to Hazel. "You, your brother, and your pa are all good things in my life," she whispered. "And someday I'll tell you about the woman who made this all possible."

She kissed her daughter's forehead. Yes, she had much to be thankful for, and she would embrace every good moment granted to her for as long as she lived.

Another Mail Order Bride Romance
by Ruth Ann Nordin

Eye of the Beholder

Mary Peters despairs that she will never get married. At nineteen, she has no prospects of finding a husband, so she takes matters into her own hands and becomes a mail order bride. When she arrives in Omaha, Nebraska to meet the man she's due to marry, he takes one look at her homely appearance and rejects her.

But fate has other plans for Mary, for Dave Larson happens to be nearby and figures she will make a suitable companion to help him on his farm. Though she is stunned that someone as handsome and as kind as Dave would ask her to marry him, she accepts, realizing that this marriage of convenience will not bear the fruits of love. Love, after all, is for beautiful women. Isn't it?

A Mail Order Husband Romance
by Ruth Ann Nordin

A Husband for Margaret

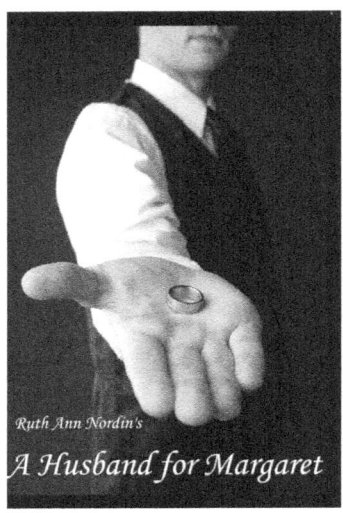

When Margaret Williams posted an ad for a husband, she expected Paul Connealy to arrive, but instead, his older brother Joseph came...and he brought four children with him.

Made in the USA
Monee, IL
06 August 2022